CITY OF O

C.M. TAYLOR

MORE BOOKS FROM RETREAT WEST

Winner 2020 Saboteur Award Most Innovative Publisher

www.retreatwest.co.uk

Novels

As If I Were A River by Amanda Saint

Unprotected by Sophie Jonas Hill

Remember Tomorrow by Amanda Saint

One Scheme of Happiness by Ali Thurm

Short Story Collections

Separated From The Sea by Amanda Huggins

This Is (Not About) David Bowie by FJ Morris

Soul Etchings by Sandra Arnold

Scratched Enamel Heart by Amanda Huggins

Anthologies

Nothing Is As It Was (raising funds for Earth Day Network)

The Word For Freedom (raising funds for Hestia)

No Good Deed (raising funds for Indigo Volunteers)

ALSO BY C.M. TAYLOR

Premiership Psycho

Group of Death

Staying On

Light

For an exclusive free novella unavailable anywhere else visit

cmtaylorstory.com

For Anna and for Andy Holland, as before

AUTHOR'S NOTE

The first draft of this book was written in the spring and summer of 1999. I'd jacked in my London media job and wangled a rent free villa in rural Spain. For some months I lived there alone. It's the stuff writers are supposed to do and it felt all proper. The local booze was cheap and the food was good and I wheezed up and down the mountains on an old borrowed push bike. I saw owls and an eagle and dozed in olive groves. But still my head was full of city. Then the NATO intervention in Kosovo kicked off and this book was written with Sky News on the TV in the other room. My younger self had issues with the TV news, with war as entertainment. He didn't have a computer though; this beast was written with a pen. Yep, a pen! Imagine that. That's the twentieth century for you.

:

The son arrived first at the bombed factory. His breath was hot and desperate in his throat as he searched amongst the toppled walls. The night was hot and the building still burned and looking up through the blackened rafters he saw that the moon was orange, seemed coated in fire like the earth.

He found them both, their cleaners' coats melted across their chests and arms. A girder lay kinked across his mother's neck and his fury tried to lift it. But he could not make the girder move and the metal cut his hands.

The villagers came, and they dragged the son from the factory and still it was hot and the fires were in the rubble and still the moon was orange and high.

The son fell forward, fell to his knees, and they stood him up and dosed him with brandy and then passed the bottle around. The click of the insects seemed nervy and sharp and the people cried and pressed notes to the son's bloody hands.

Some villagers turned and moved off sadly through the brush; others stayed and coaxed the son to return. But he stood still and said nothing; he stood so long that reluctantly, in time, all save one of the villagers departed.

The villager who stayed was called Jane. She called the son by his name and asked him to leave with her, to come to her home. But the son just stared ahead. The son felt alone at the broken factory. He felt hungry and numb and the air was peppery with dust. He stared at the rubble. Grief crashed down on him.

A man stood up from inside the rubble. He was unharmed, clean, other-worldly. The man was stout and short and dressed in black. He turned his head and saw the son. The man pointed right at him and then turned and began to walk away, across the mounds of brick slowly towards the brush. The son wanted to follow the stout man, but he did not move and instead watched the man disappear into the brush, in the direction of the City of O.

There was a sound behind him and the son looked back to the factory. The rubble was moving again. A hand emerged from beneath a pile of brick, an arm clothed in bright colours.

Quickly, a whole figure emerged; a giant, smiling, laughing at nothing, holding a huge sack, a flamboyant codpiece jutting from his flowing, bright harlequin trousers. The giant blinked and grinned.

Another figure stood up from the rubble; this one smaller, the size of a normal man, a spade of beard jutting down from a stern philosopher's face to rest against the neck of his harlequin frock coat. The giant turned and slapped the bearded figure heartily on the shoulders, lifting dust from his coat.

The grieving son watched transfixed as two more figures emerged from the rubble: a woman, tall, knife-thin with a sullen face, wrapped by a dark harlequin cape; then a man, slight, bespectacled, wearing a three-piece harlequin suit topped with a bowler hat. The slight man smoothed the woman's cape with agile fingers as she stared into the night. A black tulip swayed out from the crown of the slight man's bowler hat.

The harlequins did not see that they were being watched. The giant harlequin even looked straight at the son, but he did not seem to see him.

The son saw the slight harlequin in the three-piece suit point into the brush in the direction of the desert, the opposite route to that which the stout solo man in black had taken.

A small animal appeared from the rubble. It had a cat's body, a girl's face and a huge, plumed tale. It shook the dust from its coat and leapt towards the giant.

The harlequins moved across the rubble and away from the factory: the giant ahead with his cat, both skipping side-to-side, and the woman at the rear, silent and lean and swaddled in her harlequin cape.

The son watched them go, and still he felt alone.

1

I was early. Maybe the trains were faster, the track smoother, the city closer. Yes, maybe the city was closer. Though it had seemed far away all my life. But now I was here. And here I stood in Grand Central Station watching the people move past me. They were so white, the blood hiding deep inside them.

The bandage on my left hand uncurled and flapped down against my bag. The hole in my palm began to throb. I felt hot.

I looked at the people and I began to feel light. Adrenaline skipped into my stomach and up into my throat. I bought correctives from a woman who looked at me, then forget-its from a man who did not. I felt that it was time to walk and headed towards the exit. At the top of the steps I looked East, seeing the lip of the Colosseum glide above the shops and offices.

I paused for a moment, watching the people sweep past me. I smiled. Finally, I was where I had wanted to be. But I had nowhere to go. Out of the throng a man stepped towards me, he was stout and heavy and dressed in black. A white letter *A* danced on his shoe.

He handed me a scrap of paper and walked on. The paper had writing on it. I read the words *Join the Boundless*. An address was written below the words. I read the address and put the paper into my pocket. Fresh to the city, already I had an invite.

I walked the streets. My movement was out of step, village-slow, clumsy; I banged into the city-fast people. Then I relaxed, relinquished I suppose, and took their strides. I was happy and vacant and alone. I walked for a long time in this way.

The greatest of all walkers, they used to call me... But none of that now. Now I was here.

The streets were packed, side streets and main both full of people moving fast, trying to at least within the brimming streets. Above them all, nets strung between the buildings, a handful of distant figures swinging free high above the city. Here the past was dead: there was no why in this city of orphans, just the now. And now I had an invitation to join the Boundless.

When I grew tired of walking, I hailed a cab, climbed inside and it took me across the city. We arrived, and because I was young and because I had red country cheeks the driver charged me too much. I let him. I climbed from the cab and stood outside the house. A cat walked towards me then slinked around my legs. It was always the same: I was a magnet for animals and imbeciles. I rang the bell and waited.

I looked around, noticing the slick cars and bay windows of a wealthy area. I felt a fumbled pressure in my head then a voice said, "Hello." The door clicked open and I walked in. A complex spiral staircase twisted up above me; sleek marble stairs and wrought iron banisters. I walked it, checking the numbers on the doors. I found the flat and knocked. I waited for a while then the door opened – a beautiful face with question marks for eyebrows.

"Hi, I'm Juan."

"You're early. Come in"

I entered. We walked down the hall. She was wearing excellent trousers. I asked her name.

"What are you going to do with it?"

"Call you it."

"Not too much?"

"Not too much, no."

"I'm Cassie. I'll get Sarah."

"Sarah?"

"You're in her flat."

I sat down on the sofa, facing towards a window covered by a slatted blind. The room was huge and cream and four more doors led off from it. I stood and walked to the blind. Lifting it, the city's neon brushed my eyes.

To the West of the flat rose the honed white limbs of King's College Chapel and the petalled pods of the Sydney Opera House. Looking South I saw the drear hulk of the Pergamon Museum, into which all history had rushed, to make itself available. I came around, into this flat. Cassie was moving from room to room. Too busy to smile, precious and serious. She was stupid with self-importance. But what did I know? She'd only just answered the door to me. Who did I think I was? Calling a girl with excellent trousers stupid? I was the one who was stupid. I turned to see that another woman had entered the room.

"Hi, I'm Sarah, I'm holding out my hand, so you can kiss it. Or you can kiss my cheek if you prefer."

I kissed her cheek.

"You are young, though. Did Alex send you here?"

"Who's Alex?"

"He wears an A."

"Oh yes, it was him. Alex sent me here."

"So like him. Talent spotting. Did he find you at the airport or at the station?"

"The station."

"Well, Alex must think you're gifted. He only sends people who are gifted. I'm glad you came. It *is* early for you to be here, though."

"The journey was quick. The city's closer than they said."

"Yes. It is. The city's getting closer all the time. It's moving in, getting further from the sea."

"I've never seen the sea."

"I'll take you Juan."

Good. I wanted to be taken, wanted to be accepted.

Sarah disappeared into the hall and I looked across to see Cassie still moving in and out of doorways, still busy with things I did not understand. She paused for a moment, "I'm going to change. Let Bob in when he comes."

I sat for a while and found that I was thinking. I stopped and searched for the visuals. Immigration most channels: then war, well-dressed air strikes. Clean footage. Slick movie. Then faces. I flicked. Medical channel, an operation: green sleeves in red holes. Better. Flick. Sport. Crabs sidling across roads. Ancient Egypt. Car crashes. I kept flicking. Then a strange pressure in my head, like someone trying to reach me, some agitation, and then the doorbell rang. I guessed this was Bob and walked over to answer it. The screen showed a man with a large nose. He was dressed impeccably. I buzzed him in the door and a few moments later into the flat. He glanced around the room to see if anyone else was there, then he nodded at me in a way suggesting he was unsure if I was a guest or a servant. He went over to the drinks table, his left leg twisting awkwardly as he walked. "Where's Sarah?"

"She's around."

I turned away and heard him fix a drink. I heard the poured water swerve round shoulders of ice, moving to the bottom of his glass and I looked out of the window. He limped towards me and sat down on the sofa. I turned the visuals off.

"So..."

"... Juan."

"What do you do for a living?"

"I only arrived today."

"Organic meat. Cassie will be pleased."

"She didn't seem to be."

"Indifference is her seduction technique."

"What does she do?"

"She's an artist?"

"What kind?"

"Various."

"So," I thought I'd better ask him, "What do you do for a living?"

"Crack new markets... Say, Jono, you're unemployed, right. Come into the office, might have something for you." He moved a small silver baton across my eyes and I felt his numbers move into me, "Think me. Let's do some."

Cassie emerged. She came over to us and smiled at Bob, saying his name almost silently. He blinked and gave a small nod. Then she held out her hand to me, "Juan, come into the plastic room. We've arranged a welcome present for you."

We walked across the lounge and into the room nearest to

the kitchen. It was huge and empty except for a large reclining chair and two naked people. Cassie turned to me, "They're plastics, you're going to get your face done. But I'm first." She sat down and the plastics moved towards her, "Nose," she commanded.

I saw that their palms were glowing silver. She closed her eyes and they placed their hands in a stack on her face. The silvery glow increased until it covered all of Cassie's face. The plastics were smiling. They raised their hands slightly and then quickly pulled them away. Cassie opened her eyes and stood. A mirror appeared in the wall, she walked over to it, and examined her nose. Her nostrils had been stretched. She turned and smiled and guided me over to the chair, "He'd like his eyes done, that green doesn't match his hair. And make his skin whiter, the red makes him look like a farmhand."

When it was over I walked to the mirror. My eyes were blue now. I liked them. My skin was white. I liked it also. Cassie placed her hand on my shoulder and turned me to face her. She scrutinised my face. I couldn't tell if she liked the changes, but she took my hand, leading me into an adjacent room.

Cassie said, "Begin," and what I thought were walls turned out to be screens. Rippling blue images filled the room and my body began to feel light. I looked over at her.

"Move your body or you'll drown," she said, as she moved hers. I felt a little stupid but pushed out with my arms. My feet came off the floor and I moved forward. Then I kicked my legs out behind me and moved forward again. I reached the end of the room and stopped, turning my back to it and kicking gently with my feet. My clothes began to feel wet. I looked at Cassie, she was smiling.

"I'm swimming," I said to her. "Swimming." I began to feel good. And now Cassie swam close to me and said, "Change."

The blue screens rolled; a lighter blue with patches of white. My clothes were dry now and they rushed against me. I looked down and the city was beneath me, rushing, rushing upwards; the neon glow and the old and the new towns pushing up to me and getting closer. Because the blue was the sky and the white was the clouds and I was falling.

I felt something above me. Then Cassie floated down level with me, and we were together – attached to nothing, floating in the bubble of the Boundless. Me with my new eyes and my plastic city pallor and Cassie beside me, suspended in nothing by nothing. I reached into my pocket with my one good hand and felt for my correctives.

ONE

The sun was hot already when it rose above the dunes. Alberto was awake, the tulip in his hat turning slowly to face the sun as he kindled the embers of the previous night's fire. He lowered a coffee pot onto a stone in the centre of the fire.

Louis awoke and brushed sand from his beard, squinting at the rising sun and steadying himself as he prepared to sit up. Sansu awoke too and shivered, deep scars visible on her arms before she wrapped a harlequin cape around herself. The giant Gargantua opened his eyes and let out a lion's yawn which pulled the growing flames towards his mouth. The girl cat crawled out from his shirt and stretched in the sunlight. He pulled its feathers and kissed it.

Gargantua walked behind the dune and in a moment his happy voice boomed out, "I'm pissing a river Alberto. You could drown three midgets in my stream."

Louis exhaled long-sufferingly. Alberto smiled as he pushed a stick into the fire and fished out the steaming coffee pot. Sansu stared into the desert, smoking and smiling distantly. She produced a small, black book from her cape and began to scratch tiny words on an empty page. Gargantua came back and they all sat down to drink coffee. The giant poured a large dose of brandy into his tin mug and laughed. Louis scowled at him. Alberto set about preparing breakfast; he boiled some water, took some rice from Gargantua's sack and added it to a cooking pot.

"Well Alberto, what do we do today?" asked Louis. "We walk, we find Juan."

"We would be better served raising an international army of workers," asserted Louis in rehearsed, indignant tones.

"More coffee," demanded Gargantua.

Alberto poured and turned to Louis, "No, one by one, we agreed." Alberto turned to Sansu, "Will you eat today?" She didn't respond. "Sansu, I ask you."

Sansu nodded but she continued to look out across the dunes.

They finished their meal and cleared up the camp; Alberto kicking over the ashes of the fire while Gargantua did many press-ups and laughed, the girl cat sitting on his back. They set off to walk – climbing over dunes and rolling down them, Louis at the back, debating with himself, and Sansu at the front, moving with loping, elegant strides. The sun leered down in their faces as they followed it across the sand. Gargantua chatted with Alberto about space travel. He claimed to have designed a rocket which was powered by eggs. The girl cat purred on his shoulder.

Vapours of heat lifted from the sand, adders charmed from baskets. Two palm trees appeared on the horizon, inviting them to shade. Gargantua did a somersault, as did his cat, which landed neatly back on his shoulder. Sansu reached the trees first and saw a small pool of water curling between them. Two camels drank at the pool. They were wild and hissed as the travellers approached. The troubadours rested for a while in the shade and ate the remains of what they had cooked for breakfast.

Louis sat on his own, reading a thick old book. Gargantua moved over to him and asked him what he was reading. "Of man's inhumanity to man," replied Louis.

Gargantua nudged him hard in the ribs, adding to it, "There's another page for you, Beardo."

Louis hit the giant who laughed and picked Louis up by the coat, swinging him round. Louis spewed oaths until Alberto intervened and coaxed the giant to cease revolving the philosopher.

"Why do you study this?" asked Gargantua when Louis had recovered from his dizziness.

"It is the condition of the world," replied the stern philosopher. "The worst always govern the best. It is what we must overcome," he added, clenching his fists with intense defiance.

Sansu and Alberto looked at each other and smiled.

Gargantua stood up and assumed his debating posture, his codpiece jutting forward. "No, I put it to you that the world is splendid and full of joy. People eat, they make love, babies are born. There is kissing and music. People drink and they piss. It is simple. We have our bodies, they are made for pleasure. To each is available happiness; all seek and sin and learn. That is the condition of the world, my stupid, morbid friend."

Louis stood up, smacking his lips with his tongue as he readied them for rhetoric, "No, my naive friend, some live in prisons created by others. Many toil, while few take the fruits of that toil. To few are available the joys of happiness. Some men are dogs. Others are kings. Look around you." Louis wafted his hand, invoking the gravitas of the horizon.

"I see only sand, you buffoon."

Louis snorted through his nose and his beard quivered for a moment in his nostril breeze. He rushed at Gargantua, his face screwed up with anger. But Gargantua put out his arm and placed his hand on Louis' head, keeping him at a safe distance. Louis swung many blows, but all missed. Gargantua improvised a song as he restrained the raging philosopher:

> *Oh, he reads so much, and he gets it wrong,*
> *He is so weak, and I am so strong*

Alberto whispered to Sansu who stood and walked over to the camels. She knelt close to them and again they began to hiss. Sansu looked into their eyes and began to move her hands in front of her face, miming the scuttle of the scorpion. The camels grew still. She roped their necks and brought them over to Alberto. He pushed his spectacles flush to his nose, "Gentlemen, your attention."

Louis stopped swinging at Gargantua and the giant lowered his hand. "I propose a test." They eyed him warily. "A camel race. You see those dunes over to the West?"

They both looked, turned back to Alberto and nodded. "Race round there and back. If Louis wins, the world is black, if Gargantua wins, it is white. Whoever cheats cooks for a week. Agreed?"

They again both nodded and reluctantly walked towards their camels. There was a squabble over who got the healthier looking beast which was settled by Sansu who suggested that Louis had it because he was less likely to win.

"Pah," cursed Louis with faux indignance. But he did not refuse the camel.

They mounted and Alberto shouted, "Go."

The giant and the philosopher made off and Alberto and Sansu sat down. "Peace," sighed Alberto and he and Sansu laughed. They began a game of chess.

The great philosopher took an early lead, his frock coat flapping out behind him and his body bouncing up and down on the rolling hump. The giant was behind, his cat clinging to his left shoulder and his legs dragging along the ground and slowing his camel. He leaned forward and whispered in the camel's ear and it picked up speed a little. His codpiece jolted into the camel's neck and he grimaced.

They rounded the first dune where Gargantua knew Alberto could not see him. He whispered to the plumed cat and it made a huge leap and landed, its claws sticking deep into the flank of Louis' mount. The camel veered off course, running away from the dune. Gargantua laughed loudly, which was a mistake because Alberto heard this and smiled, "He's cheating."

The cat jumped from Louis' camel and scuttled back towards Gargantua's, leaping back on to his shoulder, its feathers pluming out behind as they increased the pace. Gargantua began to enjoy the ride, but as he came behind the second dune, he was deftly struck on the back of his head. He looked down to see a book falling to the sand, then behind him to see an angry Louis and an angrier camel gaining ground on him.

"Ha, you fool. Getting what you deserve," shouted Louis.

"He's cheating as well," said Alberto. "Excellent, no cooking."

The camels were level as they appeared from behind the

dunes. Gargantua and Louis bobbed and swayed atop their mounts and the camels ran faster and faster. They were both out of control now, and still level. They made the oasis and could not be stopped, rushing right past Sansu and Alberto.

Some minutes later they appeared again, both without their camels. They were arguing and slapping each other as they arrived beneath the palms.

"I was first by three hundred and seven metres," said Gargantua.

"Alberto, it was plainly I," asserted Louis.

"I'm sorry. I wasn't looking," said Alberto and he and Sansu giggled. "I'm sure it was a draw."

"It wasn't," they both said and turned to face each other.

"I am the better man," said Gargantua.

"You fool, it is I," replied Louis.

Alberto entered the fray, "Well, I don't know who the better man is. But you both cheated."

They looked at Alberto, ashamed, briefly in sympathy.

The argument raged all afternoon as the four harlequins walked through the desert. The philosopher and the giant were up ahead: "Life is a garden" ... "No, it is a prison" ... "To own is a blessing" ... "No, it is theft."

Alberto and Sansu walked behind and Sansu sang to the gentle one. Her voice was sweet and moved out across the desert, slipping for miles across the shoulders of the dunes. Alberto turned to Sansu, hesitancy detectable in his small face, "Do you think we'll find him, Sansu?"

She nodded and continued to sing.

They spent that night at another oasis, sleeping beneath four tall palm trees.

2

I awoke early in a huge bed. I was alone and light came in from a picture window. The night before twisted through my mind. Sarah came in. "Morning Juan. The beach has arrived. Get up, I'll take you."

"Is Cassie coming to the beach?"

"No. She has some business."

"Sarah, why are you being so kind to me?"

"I'm kind. No suspicions. You're Boundless."

We left the flat and walked down the staircase and out of the front door. It was very hot. We took a cab and drove through the city. "Where is this beach, lady?" asked the driver.

"Near the Sagrada Familia."

A mile beyond the Sagrada, a line of skyscrapers moved into view, curling in a semicircle around what we guessed was the beach. Between the scrapers we could see a huge white statue, the wide, art deco arms of Christ the Redeemer. The cab got snared at lights and I suggested to Sarah that we walk the last part of our journey. She turned to me, apprehensive,

"Do you think it will be alright?" I reassured her, and thrilled and decided she said, "Okay, I'll try."

We paid and climbed out of the cab. The pavement was hot, and although it was morning, the sun was directly overhead – it looked like the beach had it fixed at midday. Sarah placed her hand in mine. I felt happy at the slenderness of her knuckles and I squeezed her hand twice.

Above the streets, nets were strung between buildings. I looked up at them and Sarah said, "Boundless use it to swing the city."

A single road pushed straight through the scrapers and down to the beach. Shops lined the road selling beach paraphernalia. We walked down and came level with the scrapers which curled against the lip of the beach. Then we made the sand.

The sea fanned out forever and yet found time to roll into the shore. The sand was soft and sieved and felt fine on the bottom of my feet. It was too hot. We moved to a patch of beach with cooling. Vendors crawled out of the sea and Sarah bought two waters. I felt good. We took off our clothes and went into the sea. The water was not as fresh as it had been in the image pool. It was drier and less realistic. Still, it was good to be here with Sarah. The waves crashed over us and Sarah didn't seem to think of her hair. The owners of the beach had provided some fish and they swam between us. I began to love Sarah.

We walked back onto the beach and Sarah was laughing as she lay on her towel. She looked good. I told her. She laughed but I could see that she was pleased. Sarah pointed across the beach to a dishevelled group of people crouching in a circle near the water's edge, "Intrans."

A couple of Boundless came over to see if we wanted to

screw. Sarah declined and they made their way down to the sand to join a group of friends. We watched them. "They all multi-task," Sarah explained. "They'll do anything to anyone. Anyone who's Boundless."

I watched them for a while as they began to contort and ebb into a ball of pleasure. I wanted to join in. Sarah looked bored as she watched. An old woman approached and sat next to us on the sand. Sarah looked over to her, "She's an Extra, looks safe though. Let's talk to her." Sarah turned to the old woman, "What can you do?"

"I'm not your normal Extra, busking to the Boundless, Love."

Sarah laughed, "So you can't do anything."

"I can read your fortune."

"You're in finance?"

"No, I tell the future."

Sarah looked scared, "Then tell it to leave. I know the future; thousands of moments like this, but different from this. Thousands of moments that have nothing to do with each other, nothing to say to each other. The future is now, only then."

The Extra stood and shrugged and walked off.

We lay back on the sand in silence. The sun was way too hot so Sarah brought it down for us. I asked her to take it right down. I thought a sunset might cool her off. Maybe it would make her happy. The old Extra had walked off with Sarah's smile.

"Look at the sun, Sarah." But she didn't so I did. It moved slowly down onto the water, bleeding on it. I wanted to be like Sarah, so I got bored of it too.

"Shall we go and get some food Juan?"

Outside the restaurant, Sarah paid the driver. A cat came

up to me and I stroked it. We went inside. A man greeted us and took us to our table. We sat down and a screen hovered over while we waited. It was trimmed with orchids and tuned to battle. Sarah excused herself and I did some war. She returned from the toilet with different hair which I said I liked. I wanted to ask Sarah about the Extras and the Intrans but didn't know if I should. Was it bad for a Boundless to be interested in them? I asked her anyway.

"Extras are disposable, broken people. They are mad, alone, practically useless. If it wasn't for their menial functions we'd cull them all."

"And the Intrans?"

"The Intransigents are a little different. They're useless too, but they've got reason, or think they have. They're not broken like the Extras, they could seriously earn if they wanted to, but they choose not to. Can be dangerous. They have grudges. I've met some very smart Intrans who could have been Boundless, but they won't let go. They say they're against the city, but in most cases, they're only against themselves. There are far more Extras than Intrans. To be an Intrans is too hard, it makes you bitter and angry.' Sarah paused, smiled. 'I mean... How could you oppose the city, what could you do? We've offered to make the Intrans fashionable. They just don't want it."

I asked Sarah if that was it: Extras, Intrans and Boundless? She explained about the Shapers, "The Shapers are above the Boundless. The Boundless move with the city, but the Shapers move faster than the city and they make it. Alex shapes. I would have thought the Shapers brought the beach."

"And what was I when I arrived in the city – I wasn't Boundless then, was I an Extra or an Intrans?"

Sarah blinked at me in surprise, "I thought you knew Juan. When you arrived, you were nothing."

We sat in silence for a while. She had changed. "Juan? Are you going to get some work?"

"Bob said he'd get me something."

"Good because Alex will send some new down soon and we'll need your room."

The food arrived but Sarah didn't touch it. She said she was going to go back to her flat.

"Have I done anything wrong, Sarah?"

"No Juan, It's just that I'm ill. We all are. You can find your way back?"

I nodded. She left. I paid and walked outside, in the direction of the old district. My hand began to hurt. A small drop of blood appeared on the bandage in the centre of my palm. I looked up.

Beyond the netting, the moon had been placed quite high and was almost full. I walked down a wide straight road with spaced sodium and pockets of vendors' neon, then I turned into an alley and the lights began to snake more, to move in curves. Small side streets led quickly into each other. I was in the old town. It was darker here; the air was sweet and weary.

I walked past the Raffles Hotel and through the Grand Place. I felt I knew where I was going. The greatest of all walkers they used to call me... Alleys bred. Extras moved around me; alone, walking slowly alone. A woman's form picked out by the light, leaning back against a building, curving her back to its shape. She began to mumble and cry, staring at the moon, eyes full of solace and rapture. I too looked upwards, then moved into the shadows and leaned against the stone. I began to think of my home. I felt the stone against my back, sucking me in, pulling me down, deeper into memory. A cry rose into my throat. A cab rounded the corner, rolling sleekly through the slender streets. It passed me and for a moment I saw inside; two Boundless, laughing and drinking water. I saw my reflection on the car window. I looked Extra.

I flinched, moved away from the wall and walked down the street, following the cab.

TWO

Gargantua awoke first and yawned so deeply that the four tall palm trees beneath which the troubadours had slept bent towards him.

"I feel very strange today," he said as he picked up the plumed cat and scratched his head with its claws. "Like I died and was reborn in the night." But he didn't let this feeling worry him and he began his morning press-ups.

Louis awoke next, also feeling odd. "Like a library was dropped on me, then lifted," he mused as he opened his first book of the day.

When Alberto and Sansu awoke the breakfast was ready. Sansu was implored to eat but she refused, though she confessed to feeling agitated, like she had not smoked for three days.

After breakfast, the four began their trek across the desert. The day was hotter than the last and Louis felt that he was melting. Gargantua however insisted that his every fourth step was a somersault and he sang of the joys of the "feisty harbour girls", while the girl cat, smiling on his shoulder, accompanied him on a miniature accordion. Alberto and Sansu walked behind, talking with great seriousness. Soon they came across tracks in the sand and knew that they had found a trade route.

As the sun rose to its zenith, the troubadours spotted a long camel train straggling along the horizon and changed their direction to meet it. By the time they neared, the caravan had come to rest by a large oasis. Forty or so camels leaned to the water and guzzled; their owners sat in the shade, smoking water pipes and playing dice. They stirred as the harlequins approached.

Alberto neared first, holding his palms up and open as he moved towards them. One of the men stood quickly and moved towards Alberto, arms raised and smiling. He wore a long grey cotton suit and a single pearl stud earring. They had met before. The man repeatedly addressed Alberto with a long and clattering title. They spoke in a tongue known only to themselves, their words short and hard.

The troubadours sat down and accepted hospitality. Gargantua joined in with the dice game, which was appreciated, because he quickly became proficient at losing money – but it was thought that he rather hogged the water pipe. Suddenly, the man with the pearl earring clapped his hands and the dice and the pipes were put away. Louis looked at Alberto anxiously, but Alberto's smile calmed him. Some men walked towards the drinking camels and began to untie the large bundles which were draped over the animals' backs. They brought the bundles over and placed them in front of the troubadours. They began to carefully unwrap them.

The man with the earring began to display his wealth: first fruits – bananas, prickly pears and breadfruit; jack and star fruit, round oranges, bright lemons; then almonds, olives, papaya and leaf-crowned pineapples, all wrapped in soft, white muslin. Next came plump rice and wheat and corn; followed by bottles of ruddy wine and murky beer and strangely coloured liqueurs. There was moist black coffee, many kinds of tea, stick cinnamon, saffron, cardamom pods and ground coriander. Smells began to circle towards noses and Gargantua began to salivate. It took a huge effort for him not to launch himself into the feast. The man with the earring began to lift some of the food, running his eye carefully across it to check he was choosing the best. He placed it at Alberto's feet.

Alberto smiled and bowed once, deeply, thanking the man for his offerings. Then he motioned to Gargantua who picked up his huge sack and placed it at Alberto's side. The bespectacled troubadour began to produce objects from the sack: a telescope; a globe; an ornate box of filigree silver, inlaid with antique amber; an harmonica which he blew in and handed to one of the traders; a violin; an abacus, and two large umbrellas with star maps painted on their undersides. These items quickly passed around the group which had formed around Alberto. The man with the earring moved closer to him and some tea was brought over. Negotiations began in the stubby language which they shared.

Gargantua grew a little bored and he and the cat walked towards the group who were handling the violin in a perplexed manner. He indicated that he wanted it passed over and pulled a bow from his belt, running it across the instrument's strings, and hopping from foot to foot as he did so. Soon a wild dance taking place. But the man with the earring and Alberto still slowly spoke, punctuating their words with gestures of the hand and theatrical appeals. The man returned to his bundles, placing more food in front of

Alberto, who reached into the giant's sack, pulling out two live tortoises and handing them to the other. The leader of the caravan looked annoyed as the creatures were passed to him, but finally he accepted and bowed so low that his fringe acquired sand. An exchange was reached.

The man with the earring appeared embarrassed as the deal was completed and he glanced around to see if anyone was disapproving. They were not and the troubadours made ready to leave. Gargantua managed to wangle a few more water pipes and the four harlequin figures moved off again into the desert, leaving the shrieking sounds of a violin and two aspirant astrologers shaded behind them.

"You made a good deal Alberto, eh? The man looked annoyed when we left. You must have got a lot for my hoard?" asked Gargantua.

"Yes, I made a good deal. He looked annoyed because I gave him more than I received."

"You gave him more?"

"Yes, I gave more. I gave him gifts to bind us together. Now he owes me. Next time we meet he must give more, then I shall owe him. We will always be bound together."

"Alberto? That name he kept calling you?" asked Louis.

"*The Man to Whom Many Things are Told*," replied Alberto.

3

Bob was already at the office when I arrived, "Good morning Juan, looking good."

I wasn't. I didn't look at all spectacular. But until I was earning I couldn't afford to dress pure Boundless. "So, Bob, where do I start?"

He nodded towards a man working at a desk in the corner of the room, "Tony runs our trading division. He's going to show you around. We'll see what area you respond to." And with that, Bob hunched off, and Tony stood and walked towards me.

Tony was a try-hard Boundless; not quite there with the clothes, not full enough of indifference to be a real contender, but he was trying. His face was plastic in many ways and his hair was feathered. He had the remains of a hole in his neck from when tracheotomy was fashionable, and a huge watch inlaid into his right palm. His left hand was missing.

"So, Juan. Business. Where to start? Immigration's a grower but it's quite fiddley. So, let's kick off with something classical – hostage trading. Not exactly bleeding edge but the rules are clear. Think you can handle it?"

I lost control of my face and glared at him. I didn't know what hostage trading was, but if Tony could handle it, I could handle it.

"Now," Tony said, "I'll run through all this quickly and then if you've got any questions, you haven't been listening.'

"Okay."

"Nearly every day a Boundless or sometimes even a Shaper gets taken by one of the groups we might be in the process of eradicating, or by the opposition in one of the wars we might be winning. It's unfortunate, but it's business. Once taken, these hostages are stashed. Usually it's not bad for them, even the lamest terror has good hospitality. But that doesn't matter, the point is to get them home and be seen to get them home. So, the enemy, as we call them, usually waits for a few hours till we put our information out: 'Ten taken hostage in terrorist swoop!' They give us time to begin the concern process, the stickiness and breadth of which increases with the worth of the hostage. Okay?"

"Er, sure," I said.

'Great." Tony moved over to the next section of the office, "Guys, we have new."

The guys turned around to look at me and waved. They were both impeccably Boundless, peacocked up in all the new male garb. We walked over.

"This is Bernard, and this is Evan,' Tony said, 'they're our Traders, you'll be working with them," he paused, "if it pans out for you here. They'll explain how it all works." Tony wandered off into the next office.

"Sit down Juan," said Bernard. I did.

"So," Evan launched straight in at me, "here we trade

schizophrenia and impotence. They're innovative markets. We're just picking off niches where we can, putting them in long kennels. The schizophrenia market's a tricky dog to walk. It's small but growing, good for sales in general, keeps people in the present, keeps the fleas biting. We're working on some voices now that should make an attractive implant for a lot of companies. The impotence market is engorging rapidly so you'll be stroking that a lot. But mostly you'll just be making things up."

Bernard and Evan turned back to their screens and I stood behind them for a while, watching them work. Their heads were ringing and their phones were busy. I remembered all I'd been told, filed it all away. Later, Tony came over, "Okay boys, take a break. Bob says you should take the new boy out to play."

Bernard and Evan stood up from their screens and turned. They walked past me and I followed them out of the office. I noticed that Bernard had some difficulty walking. We hit the top of the stairs, slipped into monkey arms, came out onto the roof and swung up for the netting.

"Where we going?" I shouted to the traders who swung quickly ahead of me.

"Thought we'd do some war down at the Traders' Palace."

As we swung over Kowloon Clock Tower, Bernard pointed out West and I got a great view of Vesuvius, its sides steep and even, vines climbing over its Northern side, and beyond it to Mount Rushmore and the CN Tower.

We moved towards the river. It was swollen. Two dead Extras floated across its surface. A huge blue building came into view and we swung into its forecourt. A cat ran across the paving slabs to sniff at my feet and I paused to stroke it.

At the entrance to the Palace, Evan and Bernard were met

by a doorman who handed them each a long grey coat and a sabre. As they pulled their coats on, the doorman asked them a question which I couldn't quite hear. They nodded and he quickly scanned their faces with a small silver baton. After a few moments, I was also handed a coat and a sabre and the doorman asked me if I was going to fly. I looked at Evan and he smiled and nodded. I told the doorman that I would and he scanned me. I put the coat on and slipped the sabre into my belt.

"What is this place?" I asked.

Evan turned to me and grinned, "Traders' Palace. The Tsar's old winter palace in St Petersburg. After the revolution, an art gallery. Now it's here. Fine kennel."

We went into the Ice Room and drank from the vodka fountain, then moved into the War Room. I looked around me, the ceiling was high and vaulted, its arches moving down to touch the tops of soaring windows. Paintings hung on the back wall. The bar was an old tank. Tables dotted the floor and around thirty traders lolled around the room in various states of drunkenness. The walls not covered with paintings were screens. They were all tuned to war. In the corner, two ex-generals sold punditry. We sat down at a table, the glass top of which was war; techno scenes, faces kept out of it. Evan explained, "We only get the hardware shots. No refugees, no close ups. They keep it sporty in the Traders'."

Stats rolled onto the screens, indicating excellent war from our pilots. Cheers ripped through the room and some traders stood and rattled their sabres. A pundit announced that ground troops were going in at 3:10pm next Monday and not at 2:30 as he had been previously informed. There were more cheers from the traders. "We are victorious," shouted one as he threw his sabre at the wall. There was drinking.

"It's nearly time," Bernard said as he stood up from the table and practised a golf swing with his sabre. Three joysticks rolled up from the table and Evan told me to grab one. All the screens went blank apart from the largest on the front wall of the War Room. It now displayed thirty or so small jets, hovering in a line, a face on each of the wings. The planes were above a desert in which it was early morning. Evan pushed forward on his stick and turned to me, "Fly Juan, fly."

I began to move my stick and a plane with my face on its wing flew forward, "What do I do?"

"There's four people in the desert. Whoever hounds them out first gets to fly for real."

Evan explained as he moved his plane forward: in return for investment from the Traders' Palace, the government let the traders fly a sortie every day; a real sortie. This was the way of deciding who got to fly it.

I looked up to the screen, seeing my plane lagging far behind the others. All around the room, traders shouted and whooped as their planes moved out. A couple of traders who'd been in the Ice Room a little too long started a dog fight with each other, they swung around and fired, missing their targets but taking out some of the other planes. A brawl started to my left but quickly collapsed over furniture. It occurred to me as the other planes vanished from view, that the target didn't have to be ahead. I slowed my speed and swung my cross-hairs round and down onto the sand. I saw a small pool of water ringed by four palm trees, wagging slightly in the desert breeze. I looked closely and saw a foot jutting slightly out from beneath the canopy of palms. I dropped height and flew back round. I made out four sleeping figures dressed in harlequin costumes. Cross-sights appeared in front of me, and with a flick of my wrist the figures were caught within them.

"Hey, Juan's found them," shouted Bernard as a bunch of planes wheeled back towards me. My palm began to throb as the figures slept in my sights. Bernard and Evan were staring at me, waiting for me to shoot. I pulled my hand away from the stick and stood up from the table, running towards the toilet.

In the privacy of the cubicle I continued to sweat. I breathed deeply, failing to control the alarm of my pulse. Sometime later I came out and sat next to Bernard and Evan.

Evan turned to me, "What happened Juan? You had them in sight. Bernard took them out. He's flying for real now."

I looked towards the front of the hall. Bernard's cross-sights settled on a small, dark block, his thumb twitched and the missile moved outwards, impacting on the factory with near-simultaneous explosion.

Bernard altered the course of the plane, sat back and lit a cigarette. The ex-generals recommenced their punditry.

THREE

The harlequins moved into the desert, taking slow strides beneath the angry sun. Soon they spotted another caravan ahead, this one much smaller, its four camels looking unhealthy and its riders dishevelled. The caravan turned and moved towards them. When it drew closer it became clear that the camels were charging, not walking. Closer still and they saw the faces of the riders, snarling as they moved towards them. They realised they were under attack.

In one movement, Gargantua scooped the protesting philosopher up under his arm and ran towards the bandits. He reached them and Louis was swung around by his shoes so that his head smashed into the neck of the first camel. The rider flew from his mount as the giant laughed and the philosopher screamed. As Gargantua rounded on the now much-less-eager second bandit, Alberto and Sansu sat down and continued their game of chess. The giant swung Louis around by his head this time, so that his feet knocked off the rider as he passed. The bandit fell to the ground and scrambled off behind a dune to cower with the first. Sansu moved her knight as the giant flung Louis at the feet of the third camel, causing it to fall and pin down its rider. The fourth bandit turned and scurried behind the dune.

Gargantua picked up the rider he had just dismounted and carried him over to Louis. Alberto took the pawn which Sansu had sacrificed to open his flank. The giant dropped the bandit on the floor and stood on him so he could not escape. Then he knelt to Louis who did not move. The philosopher was very pale, but Gargantua saw a tiny, involuntary smile flicker across Louis' lips and knew he was pretending to be hurt. Gargantua decided to have some more fun.

"Louis, Louis, my dearest friend, wake up. Please wake. Or have I killed you?"

Gargantua stood and looked into the sky. He put his hand up to his forehead and engaged in some false swooning, "I have killed my greatest friend, Louis, the cleverest of the cleverest of all the philosophers. The most learned man in the world, so wise, yes, so wise, and so loving to his fellow man, killed by Gargantua, the great clumsy fool. Louis, who always knew wrong from right, who thought only of the small man in this cruel and nasty world."

From the corner of his eye, Gargantua saw Louis smile at this praise. He continued, "Louis, I have killed you. And I never took the chance to tell you how much I admired you. Instead we squabbled. And now that you have gone, I see that you were right about all things. How could I have killed you, stupid, oafish Gargantua with no more brains than the camel which I threw you beneath." The giant grew excited and bounced up and down on the bandit's chest, "Now there is only one thing for me to do. I must perform the act which for my ignorant though handsome people signifies the greatest honour one can bestow upon a freshly killed man. I must show you that you are worth two thousand and seven of me."

Gargantua feigned tears as he climbed down from the stage of the winded bandit and straddled Louis, hitching his codpiece to the side.

"I will bless you Louis. I will bless you with the gold of my loins, the nectar of my body."

Louis felt a shadow move across his face and opened his eyes to see Gargantua winking at him. The giant, pretending not to see Louis' revival, continued, "I will honour thee with my holy water, oh great one," and he let forth a jet of purest piss.

Louis raised his head just in time to avoid Gargantua's fluid tributes and quickly stood, "You bastard, you use me as your battering ram, your missile, and then you try and piss on me."

Gargantua laughed, "You did well my little friend. We really showed those bandits."

Louis began to rain blows on the giant's chest which gave his laughter an unusual sound. Louis stopped his beating, exhausted, and slumped to the sand. Gargantua made over to the bandit and lifted him up by his hair, "Now, what shall we do with you?" he asked the bandit as he carried him over to where Sansu and Alberto played chess.

In a few moments, Louis limped over to join them. The bandit was tied up and tossed onto the floor and there began a lively debate about the hooligan's fate.

Alberto was inclined always towards the guidance of reason and thought it expedient to kill the man. He spoke slowly as he sat cross-legged on the sand, using his hands as a balance to indicate the weighting of his thoughts. Alberto explained that this was not a decision provoked from a desire for vengeance or cruelty. If the bandit were released, he would report to his fellows that though they possessed in Gargantua a formidable fighting man, the harlequins were too lenient and friends to their enemies. They would return with a larger force. They would have to be dealt with and this would involve greater bloodshed. If he were killed however, his friends, hiding behind the dunes at this very moment, would report that they had met a fighting force as ruthless as it was skilled, and safe passage would be guaranteed.

Louis' position however was very different. He stood up and brushed down his harlequin frock coat, assuming an imploring expression, which coupled with his patriarchal stance, made him feel that his argument was irrefutable. The bandit was not inherently evil but was misdirected. He had wished to steal from the group because society (having wronged him in many ways on which the philosopher did not fail to pontificate) had forced the bandit into crime. Crime, as it stood, was merely a token of misguided resistance to an oppressive regime which confiscated opportunity from the poor and turned them into outlaws. The bandit should be taken on the harlequins' march and be re-educated, thus revealing to him the many honest virtues of communal labour which was not dictated from above.

"He should be shown how to cook for us," added the philosopher, "so he can feel the rightness of providing for a fellow worker. He can start by making me some coffee." Louis finished by twirling his beard in trademark manner and sitting in a mage-like posture on the sand.

Sansu said, "I would like to slit his throat," in a low and clear voice, the scars on her arms visible as the desert breeze lifted her cape. "If we were not strong he would have killed us. I despise him." She turned her back to the group.

Gargantua stood, his cat prowling along his codpiece, and explained why he was all for sending the bandit on his way with some gold and a keg of wine. His reasoning was as long as it was specious and ran, more or less, as follows: had not the bandit provided some excellent sport for them on a long march? The bandit was "chipper," "a rapscallion," "an urchin". If he spread the word of their lenience, that was superb. It would provide more fighting to break up a tedious march in which the po-faced bleating of the preening philosopher was becoming increasingly difficult to withstand. The bandit had provided some fun and the giant wanted more. He liked the bandit very much and looked over to him.

But the bandit had taken the opportunity offered by the elaborate debating of the harlequins to slip his ties and scamper across the sand. He was nowhere to be seen. "Excellent," said Gargantua, in anticipation of future brawling.

4

In my first week I shifted an insane amount of schizophrenia. Bob offered me a contract and a suspiciously high salary. I grew friendly with Bernard and Evan and the incident at the Traders' Palace was forgotten. Even Tony stopped digging at me. Bob began to take me out to Boundless parties. He was getting me connected, grooming me for a job, the nature of which I did not yet know. I sorted out my wardrobe and had some plastic put in: my nose was done, and my cock was lifted; my ears were heightened, my arse tucked and my legs lengthened. Bob found me a flat near the Louvre and I moved out of Sarah's. I was on it, I was Boundless, I was an advert for myself.

The flat was sweet, not in the same league as Sarah's, but pretty special just the same. I was proud of myself. If only my... no, I was proud of myself. I had visuals wired in everywhere and an image pool put in the bedroom. I had some future photos of myself constructed and blew them up, placing them around the flat to show my trajectory. I had a replay system put in and stayed in for a few nights, watching myself watching replays of myself. I ordered out for bodies. I laid out for a stash: correctives and socials; aggressives, for when trading got a bit tight; and futures and forget-its for the tricky moments. My hand was getting better and I had a watch fitted in the hole before it healed over. I bought things I did not want, ordered food I did not like and arrived at parties late, leaving earlier than I wanted, to arrive late at other parties. My head never stopped ringing.

Currencies were veering everyway and I decided to buy some art to keep my cash stable. I thought Cassie to see if she could recommend anything. She said she could, and promised she'd take me round to a few places, show me some work and introduce me to some of her artvertising friends.

The bell rang and I thought Cassie up. She looked great. Her lobes brought down and her legs had been stretched to match. She was wearing an aquarium dress. She walked around my flat, checking out my systems. She seemed to be impressed. She pretended she wasn't. Sitting down next to me, she said she'd had a hard day and laid out a line of forgetive, snorting it in one. I did the same.

"You've come a long way, country boy," she laughed. We walked down and grabbed a cab.

"We're going to the best artvertising gallery in town," she boasted. "You'll find a lot of work to invest in. And," she laughed, "to appreciate."

The forget-its were bringing me in. I was in the cab, just in the cab; mind, body, all life, just in the cab. And everyone I'd ever known was Cassie. The cab slimmed down as we entered the narrow streets of the old town. Its ancient walls and roofs became skin, its history a gloss to me. Extras moved by the cab, just people we were passing. The old town was a place I was driving through; just a place to move through with

Cassie, her fish swimming and herself a place to move through.

We came out of the other side of the old town and the driver hung left towards the business district. We stopped. I took out my baton and showered the cabby in cash. We walked towards a scraper.

"Here we are," Cassie said. "The Gallery." Three white doors led off the entrance hall. I followed Cassie through the middle one. We entered a small vestibule, also white, with a door opening to the left. "Wait here," said Cassie and disappeared through the door.

I stood alone in the vestibule. A man in a blue uniform walked out of the door which Cassie had just left by and out into the entrance hall. Cassie came back. She was accompanied by a very tall, thin man who was wearing a wet suit. They walked up to me.

"Well, what do you think?" Cassie asked.

I did not know what I was supposed to say.

"What do you think?" she repeated.

I tried to work out what game we were playing.

"I call it *Uniformed Man Walking Through Vestibule*," the tall man said with a proud expression.

"Great," I said, catching on. "Let's see some more."

The man nodded and he and Cassie led me to another room. It had two people in its centre, dressed like Dalmatians, engaged in a furious argument. I walked around them.

"*Man and Woman, Dressed as Dogs, Fighting in the Centre of a Room*?" I offered.

"No," the tall man said. "These are my collaborators, Hans and Deena." He introduced himself, "I'm Box."

I shook Box's hand and was introduced to the Dalmatians. Hans was also very tall and thin and he had his ears pierced with other ears which fell in a chain around his shoulders. Deena barked at me and looked into my eyes. "You understand," she said. She was wrong.

I took Hans and Deena's leads and Box took us into another white room on the right. It was completely empty. Box stood back and began to smile. After a while he said, "*This is called The Inability of the Artist to Say Anything.*" He led me into another room, the same, only smaller. Box paused, "And this is its echo."

In another room Hans and Deena walked to opposite corners and put on some headphones which hung from the roof. They began to shout: "Ka, re, da, cu, su, li," louder and louder, "ea, ol, ix, po, wu."

"I call this *Communication*," said Hans.

"I don't understand," I said, perplexed.

"Very good," said Box, looking pleased.

Next. A video played across all four walls. A man approached a judge. He was timid and he wore handcuffs. The man was wearing tattered clothes and he had a greasy nose. The judge looked him up and down, pulled out a gun and put a single bullet through his head. "I call this *Always Look Your Best*," Box said, eyeing my clothing for errors. There were none.

We moved into the next room. A tiny door led off from this room and Box took us towards it. He opened the door and I looked inside. It was completely full of junk: an old bed, a redundant vacuum cleaner, pieces of piping, wood, old cans of paint, a chest of drawers, a shop dummy; it just went on. Box said, "This is called *Everything Instead of Choice*," and shut the door.

In the next room Hans, Deena and Box walked into three small cubicles placed in the corners of the room. The artvertisers turned their backs on us and began to masturbate. Cassie and I stood and watched. Cassie held her chin in her hand and studied the artvertisers as her fish moved around her dress. After a few minutes three climaxes had been reached and the trio returned to us.

"What's that called?" I asked Box.

"That, that could not take a name. It is such a total summary of my project."

"Excellent, excellent," I said, rubbing my hands together.

Box moved into fiscal mode, "And which of my creations would sir like to leave with?"

I busked it. "Well, I like them all. No, no, I love them all. It may take me a while to make a decision."

"Of course, sir could take them all."

Cassie eyed me expectantly, saying, "Yes, of course, sir could take them all."

I asked Box to give me a moment. Hans and Deena recommended their argument. I steered Cassie into one of the cubicles, "Help me out. Are you sure about this? There's no paint anywhere."

"Juan, Box is becoming the most bankable artvertiser around. His work is out-stripping inflation by one hundred and thirty-five per cent."

"Okay, fine, which one should I go for?"

"Which one appealed to you most?"

"I liked... Which one's the best investment?"

"I think the final one's the most bankable."

"But where would I put it? I couldn't have three artvertisers wanking in my flat."

"Why not?"

I couldn't think of a reason.

"Okay, Box, I'll take the last one, the *Total Summation* thing."

"Oh, sir has excellent taste. We will deliver tomorrow. Around three? And paying sir?"

I moved my baton across Box's eyes and he began to smile as the money moved into him. Cassie took me by the hand and we left the Gallery. We walked out of the scraper into the business district and Cassie hailed a cab. "Let's go and celebrate," she suggested, then checked her watch. "I've got to stop by mine and get changed." I'd never been to Cassie's flat before.

The flat was in a run-down part of the city but was enormous. It was high up, the floor below the penthouse. The space was one large room with the sleeping and eating areas behind small screens. An open wardrobe ran the entire length of the back wall. Cassie told me to sit down and she went into the kitchen area, returning shortly with some water. She looked tired and laid out another line of forgetive. We both snorted and I sat back and sipped. Cassie took a clock dress from the wardrobe, then said, "Wait a minute," walking behind her sleeping screen.

I looked around the room. It was full of body casts – her work I guessed. I stood up and moved over to one of them. The cast was big, it had large hands and a hunched shoulder. I thought it looked a little like Bob. I reached out to touch it and my hand went straight through. I looked around for a projector but there wasn't one. Again, I tried to touch it and again my hand went straight through. It felt wet. It seemed to move slightly as I touched it. I walked over to another one. It was huge and its arm was twisted. I thought it looked a little bit like Alex. I reached out to touch it. Again, my hand went through. I brought my hand out and it was wet.

I sat back down on the sofa and looked around. Another of the casts looked like Sarah. The roof of the flat was fluid so I thought it and it thinned, giving me a clear view of the room above. I wondered if the penthouse could see down.

"Don't worry," shouted Cassie from behind the screen, "it's one way. They have no idea."

I stared into the flat above. A woman was sat at a desk, she was puffing on a cigarette and thinking. She leaned forward. I could no longer see her arms but her feet pattered excitedly on the floor.

"Is there sound on this Cassie?"

Cassie shouted "Sound," and a scratching noise could be heard between the pattering.

I thought for a while, trying to place the noise and then realised that the woman was writing, the scratching was her nib moving across the paper. The woman looked familiar, she wore a long cape and was very thin. A man appeared. He was very small and had spectacles perched on the bridge of his nose. A black tulip swayed from a bowler hat which he wore tilted back on his head. He looked at the woman in a way I could not immediately recognise. I tried hard to reach the word... He looked at her fondly. The writer paused, dragging hard on her cigarette. She thought some more. The tiny man disappeared. She began to write again. She made me feel... But the forget-its were kicking in and they made me feel.

"What does she write?" I shouted across to Cassie. "Oh, I don't know really. She's not successful I don't think. They're new here. Someone told me they know her. She writes old school apparently; all yes and no; all should and shouldn't. Girl needs to wake up. Anyway, I'm the one who needs your attention."

Cassie appeared from behind the screen in a clock dress.

She must have thought the roof closed because it darkened and the writer disappeared. She looked fantastic. Her hour hand was high, and her minute hand was low, and the second hand, which seemed to whiz and spin much faster than it should, was high and low.

"Where shall we go, country boy?"

"I don't know Cassie, you choose."

"Okay, let's go down-market. Let's go and eat with the Intrans."

We took a cab deep into the old town and pulled up in a tiny square. Extras ghosted around its edges, muttering to themselves. A group of Intrans stood near the centre, beneath a lilac tree. They were in agitated debate. A breeze moved through the square and lilac floated onto the Intrans. We climbed from the cab and paid. Cassie walked towards a small doorway on the far side of the square. The Intrans sneered at us. We were Boundless playing at rough, they knew it straight away. I felt my heart pick up its beat and fear move behind my eyes.

We made the door and walked into a dim room. It was thin and seemed to stretch back a long way. Cassie walked to the bar, ordered a bottle of wine and sat down at a table. Groups of Intrans eyed us darkly. The waiter came over and Cassie ordered, asking for "peasant food" with a huge grin. The comment silenced the place. I felt a cartel of eyes press into my body. I began to sweat and I drank heavily. The food arrived and I checked it for sabotage. It seemed clean.

I had to come out of myself, give her some attention. "Those figures back at your flat. That's your work, right? Tell me about it."

"Well, it's simple. I take casts of some of the people I like."

"But the casts are strange. They're not visuals and they're not solid either. They're kind of wet."

"Yes, you're right, they are strange," she replied.

"One of them looked like Bob."

"And Alex?"

"Yes Cassie, one did look like Alex. I didn't know you knew him."

"Sure, I know Alex. We were together for a while."

I didn't want to probe; the subject of exes was bad for seduction... Was I trying to seduce her? Was she trying to seduce me? I didn't know. It didn't seem to matter anyway, didn't matter at all.

"Can't you tell me how you make them?"

"Maybe I'll show you."

There was an unusual tone in her voice, pitched somewhere between damage and play. We were approached by two Intrans. One of them leant on the table and put his face very close to Cassie's. She continued to eat. "Hey, Boundless, what you doing here? Why you slumming?"

"I like it here. It's good for my work," she replied.

The other Intrans kicked slowly at the base of my chair leg. I kept very still.

"What do you want?" Cassie demanded, rolling wine around her glass.

"Nothing lady, just looking."

They walked off and I felt able to exhale. I drank some more. Cassie finished her meal and disappeared into the toilet. She came back full of powders. We paid and walked outside. Cassie came up close to me in the square, "Let's go to mine."

Just four words, four little words. I liked the words. I liked the order they were in. I dropped a couple of correctives in the cab. Inside the flat, Cassie thought the lights low. I hadn't been drunk since I got to the city. Cassie brought over some wine and we sat on the sofa. I had no idea what to say. I had no words. Cassie stood suddenly and walked over to the window. I followed her and looked across the neon bubble of the city. Vesuvius had begun to smoke in the distance and the scrapers rimmed the beach. Closer, the Colosseum squatted and behind it bulked Grand Central Station, where I had first arrived. Something like nostalgia moving into me? Something like sadness? No. No. I was there, it was the narcs and the booze making me crazy. I laid out a line on the windowsill and Cassie and I raced to the middle, banging noses as we met. She laughed. "Do you want to see how I make the casts, country boy?"

Cassie led me to the centre of the room and stood me on a small pedestal which I had not noticed before. She walked away from me and disappeared behind the bedroom screen. "Take your clothes off. I'll be out in a minute."

I hesitated, then complied. Cassie returned, her clock dress now transparent, the dark hands moving across her skin. She walked towards me and knelt at my feet. She began to lick my foot.

"This is how I make them," she said, between licks. "They're not quite solid. And they're a little wet." She laughed as she repeated the puzzle I had failed to solve. "They're licks, Juan."

I closed my eyes and felt her tongue move across me. I felt a little damp and a little stupid but the correctives kicked in. Mist moved up my body. I stood there for a time that felt like nothing. When she had finished I stepped out of the cast and looked at me. I touched me and my hand went through me, coming out feeling wet as it had with the others.

"What do you think?" Cassie asked.

I felt stupid.

She bent down and pushed the pedestal away from the centre of the room and towards the other casts. I came to rest between Alex and Bob. "Can't I go over by the window, Cassie? I like it over there."

Cassie smiled and pushed me towards the window. I looked out across the city and behind me I watched me looking out across the city. I moved towards Cassie. She did not back off. My body pressed into hers and I could feel her hands move against me.

I awoke deep in the night and looked across the room. I could just see my cast by the window, covered in neon. I felt queasy and light. Cassie's dress lay draped over the sofa. It had stopped ticking. Everything was still. I lifted my hand and lay it across my chest, across my heart. I couldn't feel anything. I did not mind this. Was this pure Boundless? Cassie, myself by the window and lying on the bed, and the clock and the heart both stopped? My mind was empty, and I could not think what it might be filled with. What was there that could be in me? I moved back into sleep, though I could scarcely tell where it began. Then I heard, I was sure that I heard, scratch, scratch, scratch. The sound coming from the flat above, from the pen of the writer as she made the words that said the yes and the no, the should and the shouldn't.

FOUR

S harp grasses grew from the desert floor, trees sprouted from the sand, and as the harlequins moved slowly forward they knew that the desert was coming to an end. The dunes became larger, sloping higher and higher until patches of rock began to appear from beneath the sand. The rock cropped out more frequently and they knew that they were walking towards the summit of a hill.

At the peak they looked over into a small valley, the sides of which were dry and powdery, and which had a small river, glinting like a twisted bracelet in its base. Close to the river was terracing, occupied by almond and lemon trees, fed by long, narrow irrigation channels. On the near side of the groves they could make out the remains of a stone cross rising above the trees, and on the far side, hugging the river, a small village. The harlequins began to laugh and Gargantua delivered wet kisses to each of them, which were received with varying grace.

They enjoyed the view for a while, each shaking the sand from their clothes, then began to descend the steep incline of the valley towards the stone cross. A small path switched back and forth between light scrub then grew thicker as they moved further down. Finally, steps which were worn and dipped in their centre appeared between two groves of almond trees. They came out into a clearing which led to a small stone church. The clearing was a graveyard, crammed and higgledy with monuments to the villagers' deceased. The church itself was in bad repair, the roof was caved in and the masonry crumbling. As they approached the porch of the church, a wing of doves burst from the roof and filled the air with the sound of flight. They moved towards the door and a voice came out to meet them, "Hello?"

"Hello priest," Alberto answered.

The voice broke into laughter, then said, "I am no priest," and a figure appeared before them. It was a man, tall and stout, he wore an apron and carried a chisel and a round, wooden hammer. He laughed again.

The man ushered the harlequins into the church where he fussed around them and found them seats. "You have come from the desert?" he asked, and Alberto nodded.

The man stood and walked to the font, filling a water bottle and handing it to Gargantua who paused before he drank it.

"Font water," the man said. "My finest blend. Drink. Drink," he urged and once more his great laugh boomed around the church like a happy sermon. Gargantua liked him very much.

The church was small, it had no glass in the windows and there was little sign of ornamentation. A large stack of canvases leaned against the wall and near the centre of the church stood two large stone blocks, the corner chipped carefully from one of them. The man handed some bread and cheese to the harlequins.

"So, my friends, where are you heading to?"

"To the city," replied Alberto.

"Tell me," Sansu cut in, "is this not a church?"

"It used to be."

"And?" Sansu prompted him to continue.

"Then my friends the villagers decided they did not need it anymore. The pews were taken out and placed around the valley in front of the most beautiful views, so that the old and tired could take advantage. The pulpit was removed and placed in the village square to be used as a stage for our many singing contests. The stained glass was removed and pieces put in each kitchen in the village to cast coloured light onto the fireside, which as we all know is the true church of man. And the altar was removed and used in the village pub as a bar. It is a most satisfactory arrangement, drinks skim across it all day and all night, offering real communion with the divine."

"And the priest?" asked Alberto.

"I stayed on here to work."

"But tell me," asked the philosopher, "why did they not need the church anymore?"

"One day, I was preaching here, entering the meat of some huge sermon about this or that, and the voice of a young girl piped up from the back of the church, 'Priest, do we need to come here to worship? Can't we worship anywhere? Can't everything we do be worship?'"

"I paused and told her to be quiet, reminding her where she was. But when I tried to start the sermon again, no words would come to me. I just stood there. I began to think about what the girl had asked me. We all did. The whole village stayed in the church until late that evening, thinking about what she had said. Finally, we decided she was right. We removed the things from the church and stopped coming. Now we worship all day."

"Where is the girl now?" asked Gargantua.

"Oh, she works in the village."

Gargantua nodded and smiled and then did the same again.

"So," Alberto asked, wishing to grasp the matter in hand, "why are you still here?"

"The villagers let me stay on. I make things for them." He gestured to the stack of pictures lying at the back of the church, "Not just that though, I work with them in the groves and I drink with them in the bar. How can I know what to make them unless I live like them? Here, let me show you something."

He walked over to the far wall of the church where the canvases lay and he dragged two over towards the harlequins. Leaning them against the font, he turned the front canvas round so it faced them. The picture comprised three panels. The first was a picture of a man, reaching to pluck a lemon from a high bough. In the second, the same man was turning around and waving, a bag slung over his shoulder and a city glowing in the background. The third panel was the man returning, his hands full of notes and his face happy with return but changed, changed somehow. The colours were deep and pure and the style robust.

"Of course, I also make pictures for myself," he said and turned round a second canvas. The painting was grey, its harsh, nervous lines all pushing towards a figure at the centre. It was a young man with an oval face and feathered hair. His skin was white. He looked lost. Smaller figures moved around him, holding things and laughing.

Louis moved towards the canvas and saw that the smaller figures were holding pieces of the central figure; one held his foot, another his hand which had a clock face painted into its palm.

The afternoon was spent in conversation, and the laughter and wine flowed in great and equal measure. As the sun moved down to touch the far side of the valley, the harlequins said goodbye. Walking down towards the village, they heard the man's voice booming out of the church, singing an old song. And soon they heard his chisel, chipping away at a block of stone.

The path snaked down and down and just as the sun completely disappeared, it widened and came into a small tumbling street, itself widening as it yielded to the village square. The church bells behind them issued ten clanking chimes as the harlequins looked around them. On the far side of the square, tables spilled out from a building and the villagers thronged around them. This was obviously the bar that their new friend had spoken of. Gargantua moved towards it with swift, gleeful footsteps. The girl cat who was perched on his shoulder began to meow.

Gargantua's impact on the bar was large and predictable. He ordered various flagons of various drinks and within a minute the cat had produced its miniature accordion and accompanied the giant as he moved through his repertoire of dirty songs.

The villagers danced around him, ecstatic, saluting the latest recruit to their ribald life. Alberto and Sansu sat in the corner of the bar, playing a slow game of chess and chatting to the more senior of the villagers. Louis sat outside in the village square, beneath the old pulpit, reading a book entitled *Alcohol and the Denial of Social Responsibility* and fending off the many itchy dogs who tried to lick him with their thick tongues.

Late in the night, as Louis neared the end of Chapter Six, *Pleasure and the Intellectual,* the drinkers spilled out into the square and snaked past him. Gargantua came towards him and lifted the great philosopher under his arm. Louis tried to keep reading but Gargantua continued to dance as he moved down the street and the philosopher kept losing his line. Finally, he shut the book. As Gargantua performed a particularly exuberant swirl, Louis spotted Alberto and Sansu, walking slowly behind the rest of the revellers. They were deep in conversation. The villages moved in a drunken mass towards a small street and then tumbled through a tiny door and into a room.

The room was painted red. Thick fabrics hung from the ceilings and covered the chairs. Music played and a well-stocked bar ran the length of the far wall. Some of the villagers were already inside, laying on the sofas and drinking. They were wearing fine fabrics. The ladies were in lace and silk and were draped with pearls, the men wore satin and fine cottons. They sported resplendent codpieces.

The drunken mob were greeted most cordially and invited to sit down. Gargantua made straight for the bar and ordered more flagons of more strange drinks. The cat began to play the accordion and the giant moved into his second cycle of dirty songs. After a while he stopped and shouted, "Where's my sweet philosopher? The girl who worships everywhere. The one who made the village into the church."

A girl walked up to Gargantua, she had short brown hair and wide eyes. "It is me," she said, and took the giant by the hand, leading him towards a small doorway which stood at the foot of a rickety, wooden stairwell. Gargantua could be heard muttering, "Excellent, excellent," to himself as he walked up the stairs with his beautiful new friend.

The villagers began to pair off. Some disappearing upstairs, others walking out into the streets. An old woman was lifted from a sofa and carried upstairs by a healthy, young man. Louis was approached by a middle-aged woman with a hungry mouth and flashing eyes. He pushed her away and ran outside.

The night was cool and the moon was gliding upwards. Louis saw Alberto and Sansu, standing in the moon shadows cast by the buildings on the far side of the street. They were holding hands. Sansu moved her face towards Alberto's and kissed him slowly on the mouth. Louis ran back to the village square and opened a book entitled, *The Need for Eroticism*. Soon he fell asleep.

5

I was a natural, I was unrestrained. My bonus was growing and growing and the currency kept twitching so I invested in more artvertising, a piece of Box's called *Meaningless Gesture*. I hung out a lot with Bernard and Evan, we went to the Traders' Palace a few times and I flew a couple of sorties for real. I got the new four times a day, ordered out for sex I didn't want, bathed in water and developed new ways to spend as much as I could.

But Cassie didn't think me. I thought her and thought her for a couple of days, but she didn't return. I left it. Boundless don't beg.

The flat was getting sweeter. The visuals were mounting and I got replays put in on the replays. But Box was pissing me off. Hans and Deena were okay, but Box wouldn't stop talking, and only about Box. I exiled him to his cubicle. He kept coming out in the day when I wasn't there and messing up the flat. Finally, I moved his cubicle into the kitchen so he could make himself useful. This seemed to work and he proved to be a surprisingly good cook. Hans, Deena and I began to leave plates of excellent food.

I'd been working hard and putting in long hours at Boundless parties in the evening, so I decided to take a couple of days off. I thought Sarah and we decided we'd meet up and do some culture. I put on my monkey arms and swung the netting over to her flat. The place was in a state, it looked like preparations for a party.

I'd been invited but had forgotten about it, so booked up had I become. I sat down on the sofa while Sarah went to change and I looked out across the city. A noise filtered out from one of the adjoining rooms, then the door opened. I caught a movement out of the corner of my eye. The door quickly shut again. I knew straight away that it was Cassie.

I waited for a while then Sarah came out and we left, descending her spiral stairs and grabbing a cab outside the door. As the cab moved towards the museum district we thought a map to decide where to go. Sarah fancied the Museum of Squalor or the Museum of Shock. I fancied the Shame. That was until we passed a small sign floating in the middle of the road. We smiled to each other as we read: *The Youseum. Turn History into Your Story.* That was where we were going. We told the cabby and he manoeuvred through the district until we arrived at the Youseum.

We stood outside for a while and did some. I looked up at the building. It was small and its facade was in the shape of a smiling face. The face was young and had great skin. A hat was projected onto the roof of the building and it changed every few seconds. When we arrived it was wearing a Cossack's hat, a few moments later a turban, and as we grew ready to go in, it was wearing a Stetson. Its eyes changed colour just as regularly. A cat walked up to me and slipped through my legs. Sarah smiled.

A group of Intrans stood in front of the entrance, stopping Boundless as they went in. The Intrans spoke to them, but the Boundless just moved past. When we reached the top of the steps an Intrans stepped forward and handed me a card, "Don't go in there, man, they'll steal your brain."

I walked past. I looked at the card. It read, *Come to the Museum of Resistance.*

I handed Sarah the card and she laughed, "Resistance to what?"

We went inside and were greeted by two young girls dressed in understated uniforms who simultaneously said, "Welcome," then gestured that we should walk through. We moved beyond them and I bought two tickets. They were very expensive and this pleased me. We moved through into a smaller room with some tables and chairs. A sign read, *You Must Wait Here.* We did. In a minute another girl arrived in the room. She had the same smile as the girls at the entrance – they shared it. She asked if we wanted to go in together or individually. We said we'd like to go in together. The girl said, "Just answer the questions, it won't take long and then we'll be ready."

We sat back in our chairs and the questions came to us. They were all personal. The last question was, "Are you passive or active today?" We both answered, "Active."

"Now please just think about yourself. Sit back, relax and think good thoughts about yourself."

There was a period of quiet then a woman with the smile came in. She led us into a small white room where we sat down on comfortable chairs. She went out and the lights dimmed. Sarah reached out and took my hand. Time exploded. It was April 1492. I knelt in front of Sarah. She was sat on a large chair next to a man, both were dressed in sumptuous clothes.

Sarah and the man were the King and Queen. I was wearing a preposterous hat and my clothes itched. They spoke in bad Spanish accents, calling each other Ferdinand and Isabelle. Sarah was Isabelle. She was covered in pearls and looked fierce and bored. Isabelle winked at me lasciviously and called me Christopher. Ferdinand gave her a jealous look. The Queen began a long speech, punctuated by yawns, "Columbus, you have waited for six years for our royal approval. Twice you have had your requests dismissed by our council, who rightly or wrongly considered you a fool. But now we grant you our favour. We will give you three ships and ninety crew to undertake your journey to the Western Indies."

She smiled lazily and turned her pearls. I found myself launching into a tortuous speech, "The Holy Trinity moved Your Highness to this enterprise." My Spanish accent was terrible. "Here you have displayed that lofty spirit which you have always shown in every affair. All those who have been engaged in the matter and heard the proposal laughed at it and scorned me."

I went on like this for some time, then rose from my knees, bowed as deeply as I could and walked out of the room backwards, Isabelle waving at me slyly. The scene moved on. She was standing at the docks at Palos, her servants fussing around her. I was loading the *Santa Maria* for my voyage.

Supplies and instruments were filling the hold as my ninety seamen toiled beneath the watch of my world-historic eye. Finally, we were ready to raise anchor and sail. The first of my three ships moved away from the harbour and out into the sea. I turned back to look at the docks and saw the Queen waving at me. She looked blank and sad. She slapped one of her servants who was rearranging her dress.

There was some voyaging now and some discovery and some trading of sorts and then we returned. I re-entered the throne room. Ferdinand was asleep and snoring heavily. Isabelle stood and walked up to me, her jewels tinkling as she moved. She declared me *The Admiral of the Ocean Sea and The Governor of the Islands That Had Been Discovered in the Indies*, which was cumbersome, but pleasing.

I wondered if I could kiss her. I wanted to kiss her. Yes, she was the Queen, but she looked so restless and pleading and I was paying for this. I'd conferred no small prestige on their majesties and thought that I deserved something. I leant forward and kissed Isabelle and she responded. The King rocked a little and moaned heavily in his sleep. I was feeling randy. Columbus was feeling randy. So was Isabelle. I looked across at Sarah but she didn't seem too into it. Columbus pulled away, bowed again and then left the room.

The cross was heavy and the streets were steep. Blows rained down on me and whips lashed my back. I saw Sarah's face in the crowd as she walked up the hill. She was doing one of the Marys, but I couldn't tell which. I saw her face again as I neared the summit. Finally, I arrived and my cross was raised on the mount, the middle one of three. Mary winked at me and smiled and then covered her head with a hood. I waved at her and shouted, "Hi."

I felt a whip move across my back. They nailed me up. One through each of my hands and one through each of my feet, like you always see it. I hung up there for a while. It was very hot. I looked at the view for a while. The town was small and dirty.

Mary stayed in the crowd at the foot of the cross. There were some women weeping and some men skulking in the background who kept looking at me with sad faces. I saw Mary laughing beneath me. She quickly straightened her face out, she was supposed to be sad. So was I, or at least tragic. I pulled a solemn face which made me laugh. I got the giggles then and my whole body started shaking. The movement made one of my balls pop out of the side of my little pants. Thunder cracked above me and a little white dove larked around. Mary was getting bored and she'd got a bottle from somewhere. She started drinking and her face became red and dreamy.

I felt myself dying and it felt alright. I was hungry and my crown was itching. Flies moved around me and irritated me. I looked down at Mary. She lifted her top and flashed at me. I started giggling again and my ball chuckled against my thigh. The rain came down and I started sneezing. The guys on either side of me were ugly.

Things moved quickly after that. We were both feeling weird and wanted to get it over. I received assurances, then a written guarantee from Sarah who played the National Socialist leader. Her little black moustache made me laugh. Partition was moody, all those trains and murders. Sarah grew serious as she wrote *Middlemarch*. I laboured to complete *Das Capital* in the reading rooms. Sarah jumped under the King's horse and I fell off it. She looked funny, her prim, long skirt hitched up and her face all white and bloody. Josephine did stay that night. We were not amused. We were the few to whom so many owed so much. We let them eat cake; played the violin as the city burned; started the fire in Pudding Lane; hit the iceberg and walked on the moon.

A girl with the smile walked in and told us what an

amazing experience we'd just had, told us we'd had the greatest experience of our lives. She presented us with certificates and told us we had been changed forever.

I felt a little tense as we left the room. Sarah was hungry so we went to the Youseum cafe. We sat in silence. Sarah looked a little sick and she blinked under the artificial light. I picked at my meal and went to the toilet, laying out a line of forgetive on the cistern. We walked out of the building and the Intrans heckled us as we stood outside in the pale sun.

"Which bit did you like best?" I asked Sarah. She opened her mouth and then closed it again. We walked out of the museum district and into the old town. We sat at a table in a square and a waitress brought us water. Sarah stared up at the sky. I felt alone, like I was at the centre of something quick and stupid. We drank our water. Extras mumbled past us. Sarah stared at them then stood up quickly, "Juan, I'd better go, I've got a party tonight. Got to sort the flat out. Cassie will be wondering where I've got to."

"Okay," I said. "Thanks for today. I enjoyed it."

She took my hand and pressed it, knowing I was lying. She walked off then turned and said, "See you tonight?"

I nodded and she disappeared into a cab.

I sat for a while, enjoying being alone. An Intrans walked towards me with some pamphlets which he tried to give me. I got rid of him and looked across the square. The houses climbed up, ramshackle and close, their balconies heavy with plants. I felt better than I had when I left the Youseum. I thought of going into the office and shifting some redundancy or flying a sortie down at the Traders'. But I didn't bite on either. I thought of my flat, all sleek and Boundless, but I knew I didn't want to be there. I paid for the water, stood and walked out of the square. A cab approached me but I walked past it and on into the centre of the old town.

The roads grew thinner and thinner and the day darker. I walked into the cathedral and through it into the cloisters. I sat down and listened to the fountain, the movement of the cool water on the warm stone. I don't know how long I was there, or what I thought of as I sat, but when I left it was dark and the streets outside were full of the murmur of Extras seen and unseen. I got a cab over to Sarah's and walked her spiral staircase once more. At the door I realised I hadn't changed all day. I looked out of it.

It was the usual Boundless at the party, Sarah charming them all. I spoke with Bob a little and he told me how good business was. He'd developed a nasty cough. He bored me. I ate a lot and had my nose redone in the plastic room. A body glut kicked off in the bedroom and I stood by the door watching it. I dropped a corrective and joined in for a while, multi-tasking with great technique.

I stood up and walked back into the lounge. I spoke with Bob about work for a little while. He had a big contract lined up for me. He offered me Tony's job. Evan was there and we shared a few jokes. I liked Evan, he remembered things about you. I lined up some forgetive and ate some more.

The new Boundless arrived. He was tall and his hair was dark. His cheeks were still red, like mine had been. Sarah moved him around the room, introducing him to everyone. Bob told him he was the director of his own company. I didn't want to speak to him but I watched him as he eagerly shook hands with everyone. He laughed at all the jokes.

A Boundless called Wren took him into the plastic room and he came back whiter. She seemed to like him and she asked him a lot of questions which he answered without pausing. He was excited. His eyes were wide and his hands moved quickly as he spoke. His breath ruffled Wren's feathers.

Cassie arrived. She was wearing a dress made from rice and her hair was long and black. Her eyes had been carved so they curled up at the edges. She flitted around the room and various people kissed her. She spent a long time chatting with Sarah and then, pretending she had just seen me, came over. I was stood by the window and the neon light hung across her grains as she spoke. Her smile was just too wide as she kissed me on both cheeks. She took my hand and I looked at her. She looked beautiful. She was beautiful, so I didn't mention it.

"Hi Juan, how are you?"

"Good."

"What have you been up to?"

"Making money, going out."

"See anyone I know?"

"You know everyone, Cassie."

"You're properly Boundless now, Juan."

She had intended this to soothe me but knew as soon as she had spoken it that it was patronising. "I suppose I am, Cassie."

A jumble of hurt rose into my throat. *Why didn't you think me? Why wouldn't you see me? Why did you hide from me earlier today?* But cool jammed the questions and I asked her about work.

"It's going well. I sold a cast yesterday. It was you, actually." She laughed and put her hand up to her face to cover her mouth.

"Good," I smiled. "Hope you got a good price for it."

"I did. A lady bought it. She said you had a nice face, trustworthy she said, old-fashioned."

Anger rose inside me and I squashed it. We spoke for a while then Cassie moved off and worked the room, conducting its pleasure. I did some more and then moved over to Bob, speaking to him about work. The new Boundless came over and I shook his hand. He looked at me with something like awe, admiring my palm watch and my feathered hair. He said his name was Ted. I liked him although I didn't want to. I found myself saying, "Organic meat, Terry, Cassie will be pleased."

He looked a bit embarrassed and said, "My name's Ted. She didn't seem to be."

"Indifference is her seduction technique, Timmy," I said, with a tone like bitterness in my voice. Bob must have noticed my tone because he looked at me with surprise. The new Boundless didn't register anything, just carried on grinning his dumb grin.

Cassie came over and I bowed out, moving across the room to talk to Wren. Bob peeled off too and Ted was left with Cassie. She laughed a lot and moved her hair. He was very earnest. They walked off towards the image pool and the door shut behind them.

I took Wren home and sent the artvertisers into their cubicles. We sat on the sofa in silence. We started to but it was obvious there was nothing; it just made us feel sad. Wren left and I sat alone in the flat. I watched some old replays and thought about work, then I did some forget-its and looked out at the city, its sleek backs grazing the sky.

I thought my messages: Boundless parties; caches of schizophrenia brought to my attention, nothing really. Then a voice which I could not place, "I've heard a lot of good things about you. Sarah says you're doing well, Cassie loves you." I snorted. Who was it? The message continued, "And Bob tells me you're the best trader he's got. I've got some time tomorrow and I want to meet you. There's a little offer I must make you. I'm going to make you a Shaper Juan, a Shaper. Just think me, think Alex." He laughed and the dull tone moved into my head as the message ended.

I sat back on the sofa, letting his words climb into me. Alex thinking me, thinking me at home. He's going to make me a Shaper. These were the words. They moved around in my head, trying to connect with something, trying to find a way to mean something. I moved over to the window and looked out. The neon licked my retina. I began to make out faces behind the half mirrors of the city's windows, began to see figures walking on the roofs of buildings. And I began to see that the faces were mine; me looking back at me from behind the glass, me walking on the roofs of buildings – each face was mine, each figure mine. Alex's words still turned in me and the cabs were calling my name.

The city of orphans gave me no sleep that night.

FIVE

The village was warmth to them after the bleak and cunning heat of the desert, and the troubadours found it hard to leave. For nearly a week Alberto and Sansu arose late, spent the day walking the many twisted paths that ran out from the village and then sat in the square, the sun tilting long shadows across their chessboard. Gargantua drank and screwed like a monk; singing, dancing, and playing many games with his lovely new friend. They worshipped everywhere. Louis also made use of his time, visiting the ex-priest in the ex-church and spending afternoons with him, talking of many things. He too spent his evenings in the square, reading and following the movements of the stars.

Alberto awoke one day and knew it was time to leave. The troubadours made their preparations; Gargantua saying farewell to his lover and Louis to his comrade. The villagers made the giant's bag heavy with presents and walked the four figures to the edge of the village. Then they stood and watched them disappear. Sitting high on Gargantua's shoulder, the cat with the girl's face began to weep.

The path moved up the valley and the harlequins slowly moved along it, the rising sun on their backs. At the top of the valley they turned around and looked back at the village. They could make out the movement of figures in the square. They turned again to face the journey.

In front of them lay a second valley, greener and shallower, beyond it the land rose and rose to form sharp peaks which lost themselves among clouds. By the end of the morning they had crossed the second valley and had arrived at the base of the mountains. The land was draped in a blanket of tumbled scree and the air had changed. It felt heavy and moist.

Alberto had spent his childhood at the base of a mountain and had the slight, lithe body and still, patient mind of a climber. He was in the mountains again, moving into the silence of ascent.

A tiny, steep path twisted in front of them and they took it; Alberto at the back, pulling high air into him; Sansu ahead, anxious and lean. Gargantua had looped a thick rope around his waist and he tied the other end to Louis who pecked at the path, regarding each step as a potential tumble. They made slow progress.

Shortly after midday the sky bellowed and a moment later turned to light as a storm broke above them. They found a small hollow, a cavity in the rock, and curled up as the best they could, Gargantua's huge bag opened and stretched above them. They lay still for a long time, the sky protesting above them and thick rain thumping onto their shelter. Sansu fell to sleep and lay her head on Alberto's chest. Gargantua and Louis began to talk, the rain somehow drawing them in, washing away their squabbles. They spoke of the village, of the girl and the priest, and of the battle in the desert. Louis began to laugh, Gargantua to listen to him. The rain slowed, becoming the bored drumming of children's fingers; then it stopped.

Standing, they saw that the sky was clear and the hills were clean above them. Small streams ran around them and the scree looked polished and new. Up they moved, up all through the afternoon. Their lungs opening to the new air and the valleys diminishing behind them. Nobody spoke. They reached a peak and behind it the land flattened and sloped down slightly. Below them spread a large lake, a wet scalp beneath a crown of hills; its water as blue as the sky. The land around the lake was green and flowers nodded on slender stalks.

They walked to the lake and drank from. They heard rocking bells and looked up. A herd of goats pushed down to pasture, an old man behind them, guiding the herd with sharp whistles and small movements of his arms. The goats fanned across the pasture, some drinking from the lake, others feasting on the new grass.

The man spotted the harlequins and gestured towards them. He sat down and began to smoke as the four figures picked around the rim of the lake. They reached him and he stood, looking at each of them before slapping their shoulders with his palms and smiling. He indicated that they should sit down. Alberto tried to speak to the man, moving unsuccessfully through all his languages. Gargantua and Sansu were also unable to find a shared tongue. But Louis found he could speak to him.

The old man spoke in a version of a language that Louis had taught himself many years ago. The language was obscure, lost almost, but the philosopher had struggled with it to translate a book: the story of a tribe who had taken their flocks as high as they could go, living in seclusion in the hills. Louis felt proud as he spoke to the old man. It was the first time that his companions had seen his verve for scholarship move out into the world. He felt almost practical.

The old man stood and smiled, once, a playfulness tracing across his eyes. He began to speak but his voice faltered and his face lapsed into exhaustion. Then his hands sprang open and he indicated by mime that the troubadours should follow him. Louis accepted and the man led them towards his village.

Three stone houses rested against a slim and leaning wall. Children sat in a clearing in front of the houses and two huge pots steamed on a log fire. They neared and the children shouted and flowed towards them in a jumbled scarf. Gargantua lifted two of the children up so that they sat on his shoulders, while another two rested on his open palms. A young boy swung from Louis' beard. More villagers emerged from the houses, bringing wooden benches out with them. The troubadours sat down and were handed cups. Alcohol coughed out from greasy flasks. Louis spoke to the old man who listened distantly, responding only occasionally, his voice blank and changing. He disappeared into the nearest of the three houses, returning shortly with a small tin box. It was flecked with chips of red paint and buckled with age. He sat down very close to Louis, indicating he should hold out his hands. Louis did so and the man placed three small objects on Louis' open palms.

The first was a ring, crowned with a dull, marked stone. As the old man began to talk, Louis interpreted for his friends.

"He says that the ring was his mother's. It was given to her by a woman from another village. When he was very young there was fierce talk and fighting with the other village. The woman visited his mother and gave her the ring. She gave it to show that the people from the other village had honour, to show that they were not animals. It was a gift. He says that he has made a better ring and one day will give it in return to this woman, though he knows she is dead."

The old man put the ring back in Louis' palm and then picked up another object. It was a small piece of wood, carved with an incoherent pattern of dots.

"He says that this was his grandfather's. That it was the handle of the stick which his grandfather used to walk up the mountain when the village moved here. The marks on the handle are a map of the stars from the place where his grandfather was born."

The man put the handle back and picked up the third object; a stone with jagged edges. He held it up for a long moment, squinting towards it. The man spoke briefly then stared blankly ahead. Louis paused for a long time before he translated the man's words, "He says this stone comes from the day that time exploded."

The man coughed in a voice with a crumbled throat. His head fell forward and he began to toss the stone up and down in his hand. Slowly he spoke again, his voice sounding like ghosts and fathers.

"He says time was once still and flicked its tail only at the beginning and the end of a life. But it floats around now, pieces of it drift around, banging into other pieces which are little to do with it. What is near has joined up with what is far. And people have become light, like skins, and begin to see others as just lightness and skins."

Then the old man started laughing, a cold laughter, and he motioned to the giant to pass over the bottle which he was hogging. He took several long swigs from it, the bitterness of the liquid visible in the watering of his eyes. Then he put the stone back in the tin and picked up the ring and the wooden handle from Louis' palm and placed them back also. He closed the top of the tin and rested it on his knees, then turned to Louis and began to speak.

"He says to tell you that he is sorry for his words. That they do not make any sense and that he is just an old man who spends too much time alone. He drinks too much. He says bad things and gets in the way. He knows that time cannot explode and he is embarrassed to have said it. He says that we are all doomed. He is going to watch the war now and we can too if we like."

The old man lifted his tin box and stood, walking towards his home. He stopped for a moment and brushed away some straw which had fallen from the roof and gathered over his satellite dish. Then he disappeared into the house.

6

I paced the flat for a long time. My heart was mumbling and my mind felt as close as the city. I dressed and took a cab over to the Shapers' Club. It was in the old district, just behind the Uffizi. It was classic-columned and hefty-terraced. The doorman smirked at me, barring entrance until I said the 'A' word: "Alex is expecting me." Then he came on all *Would sir like.*

The entrance hall was huge with a double staircase sweeping up and up and wall mirrors towering and doubling everywhere. It was strange, the Shapers' Club: the home of change and it was static. It looked old. The building had been a gentlemen's club in the time that money had first moved outwards into empire, and it probably hadn't changed at all: thick wooden panelling; leather chairs near high, dark bars; rigid animal heads jutting from walls. It was Raj and Congo, railway and gunboat. It confused me.

Would Sir Like led me into a large room deep inside the Shapers' Club. There were three Shapers in the far corner, thinking calls. I sat down in a huge chair by the fire and ordered water and a pill. I leaned towards the fire; it looked like real wood, burning. I watched the fire and tried for pleasure but it looked sad, dancing and fizzing in the grate. It was cooler and smaller than the copies. Sir Like returned with my order and I coated him in money. He disappeared and I sat back in the chair, listening to the measures of the room's many clocks which trussed the space to time. I looked at my palm. Alex was late. But he wasn't. Alex was time.

I looked at the native and the victory oils that covered the walls. I felt drowsy, smothered by the room and my eyes closed and my mind turned... The mother on the porch, waving her hand at me, and back again, into the fields, the father leaning and digging and the growing and the insects all around and the sunlight falling flat on the green and leaking everywhere, and then the bailiffs taking the land and the work at the factory and the plane flying over and the...

'Hello Juan.'

Alex was stood above me. He pushed out his shapeless hand and I grabbed it where I could, moving it up and down. I stood and looked at Alex. He was small and stout and wore blue eyes. Alex was dressed in black and his *A* rested on the sleeve of his jacket.

Alex sat down and Sir Like brought him some wine. There was some talk now about how it was all going and how I was feeling, then he moved closer to me, leaning out of his chair so close that I could feel his *eau* moving across my face. "Juan, I'm going to make you. You're going to make you. The Shapers have seen enough in you to reach down for you." He sat back as he said this, digging into my eyes with his own deep blues. He was trying to gauge me, to see if I wanted it.

I wanted it. The city at my feet and moving to be like me. To be the game, to be the rules. That was what every

Boundless wanted, probably what every Intrans had wanted before they'd collapsed into resentment. My insides leapt then plunged as I tried not to look too eager. I wanted to behave like I expected this to happen.

Alex eased himself into a monologue. More wine came for him and I switched over too. I wanted to stay close to him. He outlined his plans. He was all, "our plans", all "we will". Building me up, building me in. And it was total, he had it all covered. I could not believe it. It wasn't long since I'd turned Boundless and here was Alex, the Shaper, talking to me equal, bringing me in to the movement of the city. I felt proud I suppose, like they used to when they'd done the yes and the should.

He paused occasionally to check I was with him; I was, I was. He drained his glass and told Sir Like that he'd had enough. I did the same and Alex stood. He called Sir Like over and said, "Make him a member," pointing to me. Then he said, "We start this afternoon. I'll tell Bob you're not pedalling for him anymore. Here's the address."

He ran his baton across my eyes and the street moved into me. Alex took my hand in his and then dropped it, moving across the vast lounge of the Shapers' Club. His monogram crawled onto his back so I could see it. He took a small staircase that twisted upwards from the corner of the room, and then disappeared.

I sat for a while and looked at the victory oils; the horses charging, the canons firing; new lands, new markets and the uniforms all tight-buttoned and many-braided. The fire was low now and Sir Like brought some more wood over – real logs, just burning like it didn't mean anything. I clambered from the chair and Sir Like asked me to come with him. We entered a small room and I sat down. He cut me just above the wrist and dropped a Shaper chip inside me. He healed it over.

I left the club and stood for a while. The nets above me were swinging with Boundless. It was very hot. I didn't know what to do. I looked over at the Uffizi and behind it to the scrapers and towers. I'd been Boundless and that was good. And now. And now I hailed a cab and the driver moved towards the address that Alex had given me.

We slimmed down to make the old district and then drove for a long time, King's College Chapel shouting itself upwards and the Tuileries gardens lushing down towards the river. The city spun around me. I put the window on slo-mo and looked through it. We moved into the warehouse district and the echoes began, car sound bouncing round empty streets and warehouses empty now, monuments to when money was tied to things, when money needed objects to grow.

We pulled up outside a building – high, long windows, like eyes in an empty face grimacing into the alley. I paid the driver. He reversed and I walked up to the warehouse door. I rang and waited.

The door was answered. A small woman was looking at me. She was old. Her face was thick with make-up, not plastic. She said nothing but beckoned me into an empty room. It smelled wet. Dust covered the floor. There was a single chair in the centre of the room. It was grey and reclined. She led me over and stopped just short of the chair. I didn't like her. She put her hand up and touched my chin, moving my face from side to side. Then she put her hand to my throat and asked me to say something.

I didn't know what to say. She looked impatient. "Say anything."

A word moved into my mouth, "Grief."

"Louder."

I shouted across the warehouse and the old woman laughed, "Take off your shoes."

I felt myself redden and part of me clench and ready to leave, but I remembered Alex's deep blue and braced myself to stay. The old woman began to unbutton my shirt. She threw it on the floor. Then she undid my trousers and pulled them down. She removed my underwear. The sun boomed through the high warehouse windows.

"Sit down."

I did and she moved the chair right back until I was looking directly upwards. She disappeared for a moment and I thought of nothing. When she returned she jammed a needle into my arm and I swooned and then was gone.

... A cat with a girl's face silked around my legs and I stabbed it. A giant was in the cat's mouth, pissing a river. A porch floated down the river on which Alex sat...

I began to see faces above me. I saw the old woman and Alex. They were talking, but I couldn't hear them. There was no sunlight anymore. I felt cold. The old woman pointed at my face, then my throat. Alex was smiling. My hearing ebbed in and I heard Alex say, "Good, good," as the old woman spoke to him. They saw that I'd returned and Alex said, "Juan, how do you feel?"

I tried to answer but my words spilled and lurched together.

"It'll take a while Juan. But you look good. You're going to sound good too. And we've put a laughter track on you. You're different now. You should sleep."

The woman walked towards me and I felt another needle and before I went under I saw that I was taken from the warehouse and put into a cab. Then the dreams again as the cab rocked me down.

...*A cave filled with Extras, the stones pushing down on them and a small man with spectacles sitting with them. He was a skeleton and his eyes...*

The second time I came around I was in my flat. Box stood over me. The bastard was out of his cubicle. He was looking at me in a strange way. After a while I heard him say something, it sounded like, "Juan should be back soon."

I heard another voice, higher, Deena I guessed, "He looks pretty beat up, maybe we should throw him out."

"He's a friend of Juan's. That country shit's showing his pedigree," said Box. He walked over to the narcs drawer and I saw him lift some correctives. He led Deena into my bedroom.

I lay there for a long time, listening to the humping artvertisers making use of my life. I was going to sell those bastards. I felt strange in a way that I'd never felt before. Sick and giddy and aching, horny as well. But more than that. Also, I wanted to sing, just burst out into song. And my body was itching all over, like it wanted to dance. Loud chuckling commenced as my laughter track unwound. I reached for the visuals and did some war. Chivalric metals dropping down. Slick pundits. Reassurance. I moved in and out of sleep for a while. I was hungry and shouted for Box.

He emerged from my room, "Who do you think you are?" he asked with camp outrage.

I told him where to go and made it to the bathroom. I thought the lights and they came on, revealing me in the mirror.

I was light brown; my skin was darker. I pulled my clothes off. I had new, big tits and my cock was bigger also. I put my hand up to my throat. It felt raw. Again, I wanted to sing. I let myself. My voice was higher, sweeter than normal. It sounded fantastic and I began to dance without volition, my feet sliding on the tiled bathroom floor. I was good, I was good. The laughter track generated. I showered, then went into my room. Deena was in bed. I saw the shape of her under the covers and I couldn't help it. She seemed pleased. I needed another shower.

When I came out again, Deena was asleep. There were some new clothes in the wardrobe which Alex must have left. I put them on and felt good. There was a shirt made from banana leaves, and some trousers made from liquid metal. They were tight and made me feel... I didn't have time. I had to be in the studio by seven. I would just make it.

I left the bedroom. Hans had returned and he and Box were doing some visuals and snorting my forget-its. "Look," said Box, "I don't know who you are, but Juan's going to be pissed off."

The track laughed mockingly and I left the flat, singing down the stairs, dancing out of the door and shimmying into a cab. "Studios."

We pulled up outside a huge complex which pushed towards the river bank. I waved my Shaper chip at security and sashayed across the lobby towards the lifts. I played with myself in the lift up towards the studio. The lift doors opened and suddenly there was a throng of people around me. Strangers shook my hand and a man teased my hair while a woman looked at my complexion. I was herded into a room where my skin was altered just a touch and my hair was set. People wheeled in, saying "Hi", introducing themselves, fawning. Others just stared at me, scared to come into the room, waiting outside, glazed over. I checked my watch. I was due on in ten. Nerves tangled inside me. Sweat appeared on my forehead. I managed to clear the room and laid out a couple of lines of forgetive. I heard the door open behind me and turned. It was Alex.

"How do you like it Juan?"

"A lot," I replied, in my brand-new voice.

"Now. You're there. You're what the city wants. You've got the sell, you've proved that. Now you Shape. You know what to do?"

I nodded. I hadn't thought about it, but I did know what to do: make them see me, make them want me; reduce everything to me. Take them out of what they are in and make them want only me. Then they'd change with me. Then I could conduct this city, make it closer, make it me-er. I could shape them; be their time and be their place.

Alex had been looking at me as I thought this and I knew he'd heard it somehow. He bent down and filled himself with one of the lines. I swooped onto the other. He turned around and left the room. I was ready.

A Boundless came in and said, "It's time." And it was. It always had been.

I left the room and walked across the studio, between the cameras, between the crew. I sat down on a plush purple chair and leaned back. My face grew onto the many monitors around the studio. I looked so good. I undid my top a little and pushed myself up. The forgetive was kicking in and Juan was shrinking inside me; the city, the Boundless; before that in the village; all shrinking inside me. I opened my mouth and stared at it on the monitors – a wet, sweet hole that made me feel, a wet sweet hole on every screen and breath coming out of it and the world sucking into it, the world moving into it to be masked and changed by my wet sweet hole.

A voice said, "You're on."

I said, "Hello," just said, "Hello," and stood.

I walked off the stage and down towards the camera, pressing myself against the lens. Then I backed off and stood in the centre of the stage. I could see myself on all the screens and knew that across the city there were many more tuned to me. I began to sing. I don't know where it came from, but it did; the song just came. I moved and swayed and music came up to match the song. The camera couldn't take its lens off me. I felt good. The music growing around the voice and the forgetive drawing me in and all those eyes on me. I could see Alex stood behind one of the cameras and he was smiling as the song rolled on.

Then I stopped, introduced myself, and sat down in my plush purple chair. The guest walked on slowly. He was older than I had thought, older than the screens made him and he had a red, lumpy nose. He had large eyebrows which slanted upwards and rounded cheeks which fell towards his jaw. He was dressed in a three-piece suit – old school, yes, but so well cut. I stood and moved over to shake his hand; it was large and soft and he shook firmly. He sat down and I detailed his, moving up to tonight. I looked into the lens as I said, "The President."

The President smiled.

I moved into a few questions, did some war with him: "How's it going?"; "What time do you think we'll win?"; "What day do you think they'll have democracy?" I did all that. And he was good, spoke for a long time and said nothing. The man of zero content. I noticed he was staring at me so I pushed my chest out and angled my legs so he could see them properly. Next, we did his private, making him look all family, family. I liked him. He liked me, I was sure of that.

We stood and moved into a duet, an old school ballad. He sang it like he meant it.

He held my hand, looked into my eyes. He had a great voice and was a sexy little dancer. I moved with him. Left we moved, then right, hands and feet in perfect synch, the President and the Shaper moving in unison, taking every screen in the city.

On the closing bars of the song we hit a high note that just carried on.

SIX

Alberto woke early. He leant across and kissed Sansu as she slept, then he crawled out of the old man's barn. He walked into the tiny square in front of the houses. Birds were darting and the sun was moving up between light clouds. Alberto had a feeling that they had to hurry. Pushing his spectacles flush to his nose he turned and entered the barn to wake the others.

Sansu woke first and she rose quickly without speaking. She stood outside and fixed her eyes on the mountains, waiting for the others. Louis woke next. His eyes opened slowly and the grimace which had nested his face in sleep was not dispelled by waking. Gargantua proved very hard to rouse. He had sat up for most of the night with the old man, watching the war and drastically reducing the village's supply of alcohol.

They shouted at Gargantua and prodded him but he would not stir. Finally, Louis and Alberto herded one of the cows that had shared their night in the barn, and with considerable effort they pushed it so it tilted over and landed on the giant. When it slapped onto his stomach, Gargantua awoke with a groan so loud that it echoed around the mountains for three days afterwards. The giant was not pleased to be awake; his head, he said, felt like it was inhabited by three thousand six hundred blacksmiths, all making shoes for giant war horses.

He stood and yawned and all the hay in the barn was sucked into his mouth. When he had chewed and swallowed it, he called for water, complaining that his breakfast had been too dry. They said goodbye to the old man and the other villagers and began to stride up a tiny path that pushed ever upwards into the hills.

Alberto walked ahead, his feet fleet with the urgency of the task. Sansu was behind him, striding through the mountain winds which swung around her. Next came Louis, pecking downwards at the path with a long walking stick which he had acquired. His face was full of thunder. Gargantua tumbled behind them, drunk still and swigging urgently from an earthenware pot of brandy. The sharp, white sun of the mountains rose close to them. Still Alberto moved quickly, picking through stones, rounding boulders and scrambling across patches of scree to find the shortest routes. They came to a cliff face and Alberto walked to its base, then moved like a lizard up the flat rock. He reached the top and pulled himself over, standing and throwing down a rope. Sansu followed him, using the rope with nimble slides. Then Louis was hoisted up and Gargantua reached the bottom of the cliff and jumped up it, hooking his fingers over the top ledge and pulling himself over.

The giant sat down with the others. They were on top of a rock which dipped slightly in the centre. Winds, whirling and twisting around them. The harlequins began to prepare a fire. Alberto did not join them but paced the rock, staring always at the jagged granite which thrust above them. He listened to the lofty birds who continued to sing and felt the wind push into him with many tiny mouths.

Gargantua lay on his back and huffed and panted. He drank some more brandy and began to sing. His song was melancholy and it told of a village boy who became a prince. Louis stared at the ground. His gaze played in the veins and cracks of the rock and he felt sad. Sansu stared at him but did not speak. Alberto walked over to the hollow and sat down, glancing over to Louis and seeing that he was troubled. Alberto opened his mouth to speak to the philosopher, but then he stopped himself. The flames from the fire were weak in the mountain air. Finally, the meal was ready and the troubadours fell upon their food, filling their stomachs.

They climbed again, ice and snow growing around them and the wind pushing their clothes against their bodies. Gargantua had recovered from his hangover and began to skip up the mountain, the girl cat balanced on his shoulder. Sometimes he was ahead of the others, heckling them to hurry, sometimes he was behind, pushing them along and shouting obscenities.

But Louis remained sad and Sansu continued to watch him. The giant came alongside the philosopher and began, as tenderly as he was able, to try to identify the cause of his black mood. But the philosopher insisted that Gargantua attend to his own affairs, and so Alberto dropped back to where Louis picked his way slowly along the winding path of stones.

"Louis, tell me what the matter is."

The philosopher grimaced and tutted and pulled his beard, indicating he would continue to say nothing.

"Louis, please tell me," insisted Alberto, and the philosopher crumbled.

"It was the old man at the village. He scared me somehow. He showed us those things in that small tin box, and he spoke of them – the ring, the handle and the stone. I loved him then, Alberto, and I seemed to understand him. Then he changed, he seemed to be playing with us. He claimed that he had spoken from senility or drunkenness. He seemed sick to me. And I did not understand him.

"And when I look around me Alberto, I see that really there is not much that I understand anymore. I see no centre, no purpose. I see people caught in hurried gusts, twisting, as though there was no such thing as contradiction; as though it were not possible to think in the right way. As though it were not possible to make a better life."

The philosopher tugged his beard and moved into a closed and deep gaze. Alberto turned his face slightly and looked at Louis. He had known it would come to this. He had known that Louis' purity would collapse into lament. He had to yield to desire and chance and the incoherence of men. Alberto knew it was a mistake to be too pure, to be too centred – so designed. He knew that this purity was a denial and a myth, a thing that saw the world the same, even as it changed. Louis continued as they picked along the path.

"I had always wanted to know the world, to know how it moved and changed. I wanted this knowledge of the world to quell something in my spirit; to quell the disquiet I felt at everywhere seeing the worst take the best; seeing everywhere the ignominy of poverty and the ignorance of wealth. I thought history to change it; to seize its contradictions, to wrench it towards justice.

"So, I wrote and I thought and I lived vigorously. I had

nothing except the engineering of my hope. I dreamed only of time and change and freedom. I tried to deduce the world. Then with expectation, conviction, with an alchemist's certainty, I took my theories out into a world that had changed. I explained to the thinkers and to the leaders: I spoke of control to them and they spoke of chance; I spoke of humanity and they showed me individuals; I spoke of progress, causes, certainty; they replied with dispersal and trickery and laughter. I found them to be without shame.

"You see Alberto, I am over. My time is over. They say it is no longer real to want a plan or a system, and it is certain that many have failed. They say that the velocities have changed and it is no longer possible for a man to hold all knowledge in his head. It is no longer real for a man, no matter how great his erudition or sympathy, or how impeccable his motives, to sit and to know and to think the world to change it. They would have me join a quango Alberto."

Louis had said the word quango with disgust, and Alberto could not help but smile at him. He said the word in the way that a wanted thief might say dungeon. Alberto looked up for a moment at the mountains and thought about Louis, thought of what he wanted. He lived in a world of mystery and richness, a world replete with the fabulous, the comic, the ambiguous; but he wanted to tame it, to make it like his head: straight and deep and kind.

"There was a girl once Alberto," Louis continued with a breaking voice, "and she said that she loved me. It was certain to me that I loved her also. She wanted to be with me, but in the way of these things, she was married to another. She would not leave him, nor tell him about me. I walked away from her because of this, because if I could not have all…"

Louis stopped walking and knelt in the path. His eyes

flicked around him, seeing nothing. Alberto stood over him as the philosopher continued.

"I should have drunk and sung with the others. But I chose the smugness of the sentinel, that distance from life which is nothing but fear of it. I have thought of only one thing, of when my mind would walk the earth and save us from our cruelty. But I see now. We all move with the tides. It is the sea and not the rock that is our home. There are no futures or fortresses, just the maybe, maybe, maybe of the waves."

Louis picked up a handful of shingle. He weighed it in his hands then stood quickly and threw it, aiming it at the tallest peak. The shingle dispersed and fell short, clattering against larger rocks. Louis put his hands up to his face and began to shudder slightly. Alberto moved towards him and stood the philosopher up and held him, the philosopher's beard falling across his face and tickling his eyelids. Louis began to weep.

7

I found the most expensive flat I could, it was a penthouse; rooms and rooms of it, growing mindlessly from the huge central area. It was in the same district as Sarah's and I invited her round to see it. She was green – that was the best bit of all. I had carpart laid in all the rooms and a famous designer fitted me a kitschen. I sold the artvertisers for less than I paid for them. That was fine, I still had money to burn.

I bought all the flats under mine and when I'd had the building's elevator strengthened and the air around it hardened, I knocked them down so my flat floated alone. Alex and I looked around to find a sponsor for the show, but we couldn't find. I guess the rates were too high. That was fine. My little routine with the President had made me, I was Shaping.

Some of the Alps were brought to the edge of the city. I paid for that. I could see them from my windows and I liked the view. There were some caves at the base of one of the mountains and I planned to go and explore them. But for the moment I did not want to leave the city; I felt it might die without me.

I had the morning off and I walked around the flat, looking at the view from all directions. There was no cloud on the mountains now and you could see the veil of snow on their peaks. From another window I could see the Tuileries Gardens.

There was a preplay system wired across the flat and I started messing with it. It predicted what you'd be doing later. I flicked to tonight to see what I'd be wearing, that way I could wear something else so I wouldn't get bored. But I hadn't quite got used to the controls. I got angry and broke one of the screens. That seemed to work and I got the hang of it. I laid out a line of forgetive. I snorted and my mind compacted, screening out memory. I rang and thought it. It was Cassie, she wanted to come over. She blanked me for weeks and then, when I start Shaping, she thinks me. I laughed, sure she could come over, it would be good to see her. That was true. But it would be sweeter to refuse her when she arrived.

I slipped on my dressing grown and started messing about in the kitschen, being all breakfast about things. Cassie would think I'd just got up after some grievous night of Shaping. I looked magnificent in my gown. But she couldn't have me; she could stay long enough to want me and then she could go.

She arrived and I thought her up. She walked around the flat while I dallied with the phoney breakfast. She was wearing a boa dress, its mouth cowled over her head and its teeth curling in towards her eyes. She pulled the snake head backwards and it fell towards her shoulders. After a few she came up to me, "Nice place, Juan."

I nodded and thought the floor. It thinned and you could see through it right down to the ground. Cassie looked down to the cabs skimming past and the thin elevator shaft moving down from the flat like a flamingo's leg.

Cassie nodded and smiled and opened her mouth. I put up my hand to stop her speaking, motioned her over to the sofa and handed her a glass of water when she sat. She tried to speak once more, but again I stopped her. I sat down and picked up the preplay remote. I played with it for a while and an image came up on the remaining screens. It was Cassie and myself sat on the sofa, my breakfast was nearly finished and Cassie's water glass was empty.

Screen Cassie spoke, "Look Juan, I'm sorry I didn't get in touch. I was really busy that's all."

Screen Juan just smiled.

I turned off the preplay and began to eat my breakfast. Cassie stood in silence and walked over to the window; she looked beyond the smoking tuft of Vesuvius and across to my Alps. She looked fine. She stared at the mountains. I continued to eat.

After a while she turned to me, "Well Juan, I *am* sorry I didn't get in touch earlier. But it wasn't because I was too busy. I didn't get in touch because I felt something for you."

I messed with the preplay. Screen Cassie said, "That's why I sold your cast. Because I couldn't stand looking at it. Lying in bed at night, looking at your shape, it started to do things, to take me out of the Boundless."

I carried on eating. Cassie hissed at me and her dress coiled around her.

"But Juan, that is why I sold the cast."

I took a mouth full of breakfast and did my preplay thing.

"So, Cassie," Screen Juan said, "why did you pick this

moment to overcome your mixed feelings for your friend Juan? Why now did the Boundless give and lead you here into attachment?"

I was really enjoying my coffee. Cassie left the window and slithered over to the sofa. I dropped the remote, deciding to let this one run out in normal.

"I don't know Juan. I'm sure you think it's because you're Shaping, and Alex has got you under his wing and you're screened out everywhere. That is what you think isn't it?"

I looked down through the floor to the busy street, then darkened the floor over to reveal the carpart. I sat back for a while then stood and walked to the narcs drawer, returning to the sofa with a bag of forgetive. I moved closer to Cassie and turned and looked at her face. Her nose had been snubbed slightly to match the angle of her forehead. New lobes brushed against her neck and her hair was gone, revealing a scalp of emerald green. She felt me look at her, felt the stroke in my eyes. Her dress rasped and constricted.

We both knew these games: attack and counter-attack; hurt and recrimination; rejection and need; all the stupid old games. We were both schemers, we knew that, it was humiliating to pretend otherwise. It was lies to pretend that we were more than lust and power and convenience. It was ungrateful to want more. I wanted to touch her. But first I wanted to kill the game.

"Cassie, tell me why you didn't get back to me."

"Do you really want to know?"

I nodded.

"You were newly Boundless and you were clingy. I could still taste the organic on you. You were too keen and you weren't important enough to encourage. I was having more fun dropping correctives with other Boundless."

"So why did you come now?"

"Because you're a Shaper and that turns me on."

"Thank you, Cassie."

I laid out a long line and we raced to the centre of it. I dropped two correctives and we tumbled over and down. She shed her dress and I slipped from my gown.

Afterwards she stayed and we spoke for a while. She said that I should come around and she'd do another body cast, now that I'd changed so much. She was sure that when she sold the new one the buyer would not think it an antique. This tickled my vanity. We watched our union on replay and because I had a show that night and wanted to keep my energy, we watched our next on preplay. It was better than the first, more athletic and cynical I suppose. We looked out of the window; Vesuvius plumed and a ship of cloud had moored to the hills. The drugs were sizzling in me and my mind was gliding because I imagined I could see through the clouds, see through to the highest of my new Alps. And on the peak, I saw someone. He had a beard and a stern face and he was crying, looking over to my floating flat and crying.

Cassie grew a new dress and I did some war, then I showed her out. I sat back down and thinned the floor, watching the capsule of the elevator move down and stop at the pavement. Cassie stepped out. She stopped walking and looked upwards. She knew I was watching. I laughed and thickened the floor.

I had a new song to do that night and figured I'd better rehearse it. True, last time it had just come but that was the post-op high. I could probably do it again but I didn't want to take any risks. I went into one of the bathrooms and began to sing. Alex thought to tell me the guests for tonight's show. He suggested that I come and see him tomorrow at the Shapers' Club, he thought it was a good idea for me to have my legs lengthened some more and my body athleticised. I agreed. Why not? I continued my practice.

I stopped after a while. I felt strange, like there were small cracks in my body; one running through my arm, just above my right elbow, and one opening in my neck. It had been a strange day though and I blocked the feeling and continued with my practice. I finished and checked my palm clock. I thought Evan, but he was flying a sortie down at the Traders' and he couldn't talk.

My palm began to ache and I laid out a line. I scooped it up in one and the door rang. Whoever it was, they weren't a Shaper or a Boundless, otherwise they'd have thought me. I remembered first arriving at Sarah's and the fumbled feeling at the door as they tried to think me up. I thinned the floor and looked down. A woman stood at the bottom of the lift shaft. I didn't recognise her. She looked good so I let her in. Maybe Alex was sending me some organic to make Boundless.

I arranged myself on the sofa for the benefit of the woman. A little bit of leg was showing and I felt good. The upstairs bell went and I thought it open. I looked over to the door. The woman stood there and you could tell that she had no funds. She had the red cheeks of new arrival.

I beckoned her and she walked towards me. Her eyes darted and ate up the flat. She came closer. I stared at her; she was beautiful in a hillbilly way, a strong look about her, a confidence strangely teamed with her obvious failings. She came right up to me and I felt some bubbles of past gliding up round the now. I shivered as I entertained the thought that I knew her.

She was standing right in front of me now. She was smiling. She put her bag down on the floor. "Hello, Ned."

I shivered again. That name, blowing away the forgetive. That awful name, so thick and short and dumpy; a crude wind blowing me back in time. Who was she? Nobody knew that name. I was Juan now, not Ned, not the son. I was Juan. My left hand felt like it was coming away from the wrist.

"Aren't you going to say anything, Ned?

I said, "Sit down," and then I stood, walking over to the kitschen, buying time as my memory exhumed itself. "I've been to see you before, but you were always sleeping. They said I shouldn't wake you."

"Would you like some water?" I asked. She nodded.

And then it came, gathering momentum and moving through me... This woman and I as children. She was at the school desk next to mine; then in the fields, working next to me, picking as quickly as I; and I saw her smiling. Then on the porch, sitting next to me... Her face in the blue shadows of dusk and the swifts moving around the house in zig-zag flights... We walked on a small path which was rutted with wheel tracks and thick with dust. Then we were outside by a broken building and she was crying. Then there was nothing after that, except an absence that filled everywhere like a power cut.

I came to. She was sat on the sofa looking at my Alps. I took her some water and she saw that my hand was shaking. She looked, and here I thought the word, even though I hated it, she looked kind. I sat down opposite her.

"How are you Ned?

I did not reply.

"You're doing well?"

"I'm doing well."

"Is this room all yours Ned?" She looked around. I nodded. Something came into her face and her breathing became sharper. I stood and walked over to the window; my eyelids firmly shut. I heard the soft padding of her feet moving up behind me and my whole body tightened. She stood behind me. She was taller than me, still taller than me. She brought her hands down and held me by the waist, softly, with unbearable tenderness.

"Why did you come, Jane?" Her name came from nowhere.

"To see you."

"Is it that simple?"

"No."

I broke away from her, still feeling her palms on my hips, melting down inside me, shaping me. I shuddered. I wanted to tell her to shut up but she wasn't speaking. I found myself smiling. I hated her though. She was bringing me in, bringing me back, making me real. She walked up to me and touched me, her fingers moving down from my temple to my jaw, then coming forward to my chin and resting there.

"Do you miss them?"

And now I hated her. I wanted to buy things. "Ned," she repeated, "do you miss them?"

I fought the question and lost. Did I miss them? I could see my father, his back wet as he bent and picked and bent, gathering from the trees. And my mother beside him, her skirt a bell of pale blue cotton. "No Jane I don't miss them." I couldn't tell if I was lying.

"Do you miss me?"

Again, I said, "No." And I knew that this was true. I didn't miss her. I was from another world. I moved away, like I had done before.

"I'm getting married, Ned."

"Do you love him?" The question came from nowhere.

She opened her mouth and closed it again. She didn't love him. She had some sense, but I wanted her to say it.

"Do you love him?"

She looked at the ground, "He's kind and he loves me..."

Oh, how weak she was; wanting and not finding and pretending she'd found. I hated her then. I came close to wanting her for a moment, but something intervened, some mix of disgust and pride, which once recognised made me want her more until finally I wanted her and hated her so much that I knew that I couldn't have her.

She looked at me for a long time. Then she went to the bathroom. I moved to the narcs drawer and laid out a line. I pulled it into me, all that now moving into me. I grabbed a wad of notes and walked to her bag, stuffing them far down inside it, then I reached for the remote and did war – not much, just enough to brain me. When she came back out I was standing by the window, pretending to enjoy my Alps. Or I was enjoying my Alps. I felt her walk up behind me again, but this time she stopped. "I'm going to leave now Ned. Is there anything you want to say to me?"

I turned to face her and she liked nothing in my eyes. She walked over and picked up her bag. She turned as she got to the door and I wanted her again. She smiled at me, once, with sadness, then she walked out. My hand broke off and fell to the floor. I picked it up and thinned the floor, watching the lift move down to the ground. She walked out on to the pavement, wearing those stupid clothes. She walked down the street and disappeared.

I thought Alex and asked him to send a plastic over. I had to get this hand back on before the show. Alex told me to put it on ice. He said that I should get to the studio early and he'd have someone meet me there and fix it up. Then his voice changed, it slowed and became a little serious, "Are you alright?" he asked.

I said I was fantastic, that I'd been rehearsing the song all day. It sounded just about as good as I felt. He paused and a laugh, no, maybe a sneer, came into his voice. He asked me if I'd had a good time with Cassie. I wondered how he'd known. I was hurt for a moment and then the call ended.

I iced my hand and did some lines. Clouds gathered on my Alps and Vesuvius grew angry. I changed and went downstairs. I grabbed a cab and it took me to the studios.

SEVEN

Louis had been walking ahead all day, opening his hands then clenching them into fists. More than once the wind had carried his troubled whispers back to the other harlequins. He was the first to reach the pass and he waited for them there. The pass was wide and its highest point was marked by a cairn. The snow had begun to melt and the sun to unlock the earth. Mud climbed over their boots.

Alberto suggested that they spend the night resting by the cairn and the others agreed and moved towards it. Gargantua reached the pile of rocks first, adding a huge boulder which he balanced impossibly on its peak. Flag poles jutted from gaps in the cairn and Sansu added her own, tearing a piece from her harlequin cape, tying it to her walking stick and resting it between two stones. The flag lashed in the wind.

Louis began to prepare the food while Gargantua did several hundred press-ups, his cat counting them from its perch on his back. Alberto and Sansu walked a little way from the camp and spoke quietly, then returned with glee and purpose. Alberto cleared his throat and began to speak in a soft and serious voice.

"Gentlemen," he said, and Gargantua looked up to check that he was being addressed, "gentlemen, Sansu and I are getting married."

Gargantua and Louis looked over to Sansu who nodded and said that it was true.

Alberto continued, "And we intend to get married tonight. With your help. Louis we were hoping you would be the best man, and Gargantua, we want you to perform the ceremony."

The giant ran to them and smeared them in congratulations, while the philosopher shook their hands. They agreed to take up their designated roles. Gargantua would need, he said, a couple of hours to throw a ceremony together, while Louis said he would need the same to craft his thoughts. The best man and the priest disappeared behind separate rocks to prepare, leaving the bride and groom to assemble the wedding supper; a situation which amused them both.

When the meal was ready the two came over, picked up their plates and quickly returned to their offices. Sansu and Alberto noticed that the giant and the philosopher looked far more flustered than themselves. At the designated hour, Alberto fetched the philosopher and the giant from behind their rocks. There was plenty of "a few more minutes" and "I'm not quite ready" but eventually he was able to herd them out.

"Right," said Sansu to the now-sheepish giant, "where do you want us?"

She was offered a blank look in reply, then Gargantua studied his notes and said, "You, over there," ushering Sansu to one side of the cairn, "and you, over here," ushering Alberto to the other.

Louis, it was revealed, had not only spent his time writing his speech, but had also twined two hair rings from his beard. He bent down and whispered to the girl cat and it nodded and rolled on to its side. Louis lifted the cat up in one hand and placed the two rings on its stomach, using the cat as a cushion. Gargantua placed Louis in front of the cairn, between Sansu and Alberto. The ceremony began inauspiciously with Louis and Gargantua speaking at the same time. Dark looks were exchanged between them and they stepped away from the cairn to debate the matter. After some minutes of insult, brawling and slim discussion, Sansu stepped in, "Louis, why don't you speak after Gargantua."

He scowled but she flattered him, "We will need some sense after the giant's prattle."

Sansu winked at Gargantua so he knew what game she was playing. Louis agreed and the four stepped back into their positions, with Louis holding out the cushion cat. Gargantua began to speak, but he quickly stopped and ran behind his rock. He returned in a moment after rummaging through his sack. He was wearing a cleric's robe. The other harlequins wondered about this but did not delay proceedings by enquiring. Finally, they were ready and Gargantua began.

"Fellow drunkards, noble syphilitic friends and Olympian imbeciles, today we are as blessed as a fat king's arse, for we are to join two of the best little chaps within a million and six miles. We are as happy as the tip of the pontiff's John Thomas as we contemplate the marriage of these cracking ruffians; Alberto, born as we all were from the bombs of the factory, and Sansu, possessor of the most superb cape.

"And we know that their union will last as long as that between eating and shitting, between the in-and-out game and babies, and between thirst and booze. For they are two noble characters: Alberto who would be turned inside-out rather than utter his detested unreason. And Sansu, strong as the stench of never-cleaned oxen, and as true as every word I have spoken so far.

"We also take this opportunity to draw to the attention of those gathered here the countable virtues of the best man, the great philosopher Louis, who is a serious man and wears a beard as large as a magic carpet. And, why not, let us praise the virtues of the speaker, the giant Gargantua; priest, japer, drinker, violin player; a man so strong as to knock Armadas off course with a puff of his bottom breeze; a man of such gigantic modesty that if someone were to say to him, 'Gargantua, you are the most superb man to have quaffed a jug since Hercules himself', he would deny it for as long as it took to boil seven ant's eggs.

"And so, as we stand here on this muddy and detestable little pass, after crossing deserts with more grains of sand than there are thoughts in all the worlds; after climbing mountains higher even the praise the speaker deserves for his many valorous deeds; as we stand here, ready to go down into the city and find the one who troubles us, we drink a toast and toast a drink to the fabulous couple and priest and to the quite good best man."

Gargantua moved among the troubadours, pouring drinks for them all. Louis began to speak but the giant hushed him, "Well that's the first part done, now for the second, which is probably better."

He continued, "We hope that the couple spend endless nights of bliss together, playing hide the rabbit and the two-bottomed game and generally going at it quite a lot; so that babies fall from Sansu like frogs from the sky in the many strange lands that the learned Lepommetarch wrote of in his *History of Animal Rain*. We hope also that those babies are not the detestable, whining bags of shit that so many of their like are, but rather are like myself when I was born – ready to drink many draughts and a surprise and pleasure to my wet nurse every time I buried my winning nose in her pillows.

"We hope also that the chaps of their union do not turn into soft beardos, increasing the woes of man with tidings dark enough to make the sun go down. We hope also that they do not turn on their parents, locking them inside a wooden hut on the edge of a gloomy forest and shooting burning arrows so that the hut catches fire and the parents scream louder than thunder which has stubbed its toe, while they burn to a death more horrible than six hundred nights with no booze spent in the company of twelve tuneless crones, all as dry as a river bed on the moon. We further hope just in general, we hope in general."

Gargantua continued in this way, oblivious to the other harlequins who stood silently, shifting from foot to foot, yawning occasionally. Then, at last, he came to the end, "So, I think you're probably about married then. Louis, give them the rings."

Louis stepped forward and wafted the cushion cat towards the two. Sansu picked up the first ring and slipped it over Alberto's finger, then Alberto did the same to Sansu. And they were married. They kissed for a while and Louis approached the giant priest to challenge him on the many insults which his speech had directed towards him. But Gargantua did not understand, believing he had been more than fair to the great philosopher. Louis landed several punches on the giant's nose, but Gargantua picked him up and smothered him in kisses. It came time for Louis to speak,

"I'll keep my words brief," he cast a scowl in the direction of the giant, "because I have the taste to recognise what is inappropriate. I consider marriage to be the most abominable of human institutions. Despite this, I do feel a certain degree of happiness today."

And with that he sat down. Sansu and Alberto looked at each other and smiled, satisfied with the virtuoso eccentricity of their friends' performances. They both hugged Gargantua and they both hugged Louis and they showed off their rings to the wind and they were happy.

The sky began to darken as the troubadours toasted the newlyweds. A glow crept up on the far side of the pass. It was the sodium halo of the city of orphans, so close now – down the mountain, across the plain and they were there. Their journey was coming to an end.

They slept around the cairn that night, curled around its stones and the sky above them was wet with stars. They dreamed of the boy, the one who had left them. They dreamed of waking him to dream.

8

The show was number one in all ratings: play, replay and preplay. The President had become my co-host and was proving to be an entertaining man. We ran interviews with people who'd just been murdered, reuniting them with their killers. Then the war stepped up; we'd won early and we sent camera troops and soldiers in. Screens went twenty-four on it so I found myself with a holiday. I decided to go to the caves at the foot of my Alps. I thought about inviting Sarah, but then I didn't do so.

I dressed in some low-key garb and did a bit of war, then I left the flat and descended into the city. A group of Intrans passed me, carrying banners that demanded peace. There was something wrong with them.

I grabbed a cab and moved towards the old district. The Extras were thick today, mumbling around the car; so many of them, all locked down into themselves, wrestling in hidden shapes. We slimmed down as we got deeper into the old town. We passed the Cathedral and its fat bells were tolling marriage.

In a square, a group of Intrans were clustered around a woman. She was singing and her voice was sweet. I stopped the cab and asked the driver to wait. I stepped outside – her voice was wind and fruit and sunshine. I sat down at a table and a waitress brought me a water. It was hot. A Boundless walked through the square and looked over to my table. He recognised me from the show. My laughter track boomed out as he approached. He was fashionable so I let him feel me up for a while. The tip of my finger broke off and he asked if he could have it. It was a beautiful day so I let him. He went away and I remained at the table, letting the singer's voice clamber inside me.

The group of Intrans around the singer seemed hypnotised and I felt no hostility from them. A cat walked out from beneath the table next to mine. I could see the spine of the Cathedral to my left and the bells still rolled high up, clattering out the holy union. Their sound mated with the singer's voice and I became like time... I saw some bullet holes high up above a doorway, from the time that war was earthed. I imagined putting my fingertips into those holes and feeling the rock surround them. They would feel calm and smooth. I imagined the man who had the made the holes. He was young and scared. I ordered some more water.

The cabby climbed out of his seat. Was I going to sit there all day? I paid him and he waited. The bells had stopped ringing, but I could hear them still, their echoes mooching around the old town. The singer started another song. I thought of Cassie on top of me. I did not think of Jane.

I looked up at the spire with its golden cross and I laid out a line on the table and took it up in one. I did another one and the old town began to dance around me. A young Boundless couple were sat on the table next to mine, they recognised me but were too cool to approach. The female Boundless was wearing the same metal trousers that I had worn on my first show. That was good, I was ahead, I was the game. They beckoned the waitress and she hurried to their table. They were full of complaint. Their food was late; they had things to do; they couldn't just sit here waiting for her to get it together. The waitress apologised and hurried off, returning quickly with their food. She placed one of the plates down on the table then moved around to place the other. She stumbled and the plate fell forward, the food landing in the lap of the female Boundless.

The male Boundless stood and began to shout. The waitress backed off in fear. The male Boundless moved towards the clumsy waitress while his partner scraped the food from her trousers. The waitress moved backwards and stumbled, falling and landing heavily. Her head cracked onto the cobbles. She started to moan. I began to stand, to move to help her, but I caught my shirt sleeve on the corner of the table. I ripped it slightly and sat back down. I was annoyed. The singer's voice still floated around the square.

The female Boundless with the metal trousers stood and moved towards the waitress. She stood above her and knelt to her and whispered something to the waitress I did not hear. Then she stood and started to kick the waitress. Screams rose above the singer's voice. The Boundless kicked and the waitress howled. Everyone in the square looked over to them. The waitress curled up and covered her head with her hands.

I began to sweat and stared at the bullet holes above the doorway, they looked so neat and smooth. Two Intrans broke from the group in front of the singer and walked towards the waitress to help her I thought, but no, they just joined in, kicking her. The singer's voice grew into the tempo of the violence as more Intrans came over and surrounded the waitress.

A deep crack opened up and ran across my thigh. The screams of the waitress stopped and the people began to move away.

The Intrans returned to listen to the singer. The Boundless sat back down at the table next to mine and called to another waitress who attended promptly. They asked for the bill and paid, tipping heavily. Then they stood and walked to the road, hailing a cab and driving from the square.

I looked down to the bleeding waitress. She did not move. Her dress was ripped and her hair limbs pushed out at stupid angles. I drank another water then paid and got into my cab.

The city was thick with people. The cab moved slowly through the streets and I leaned back in my seat and closed my eyes. I pictured the metal trousers of the Boundless and the howling face of the waitress. I did not picture Jane.

The city began to thin as we pushed slowly out and the plain opened before us; a huge plate of nothing, uselessly mirroring the sky. We drove by graveyards. I looked at my driver, he had a fat neck and bad hair. I hated him and imagined kicking him, stopping the cab right there and kicking the life out of him. I thought of Cassie and saw her tongue move up Alex's thigh.

The land became flat and insolent, like a huge broken screen. We moved quickly across the plain and I took another line. We approached the base of Vesuvius and I looked up to it. Smoke was waving from its crater, and small, dirty cinders that could not be sold were being flung into the air. The road began to climb slightly. I exhaled.

We wound up the road and hit the base of my Alps. We were some way off from the caves but I decided to walk. I tipped the driver and stepped from the cab, beginning the ascent to the base of the rock face. I turned and looked at the city; a model of glass pushing up from the plain, and behind it, the yellow scar of the new beach

...I saw fires falling and the city melting and being carried away on the wind like polythene...

I started to retch and crouched down by the side of the road, sticking my fingers down my throat. I threw up but could not remove my fingers. I retched again and they loosened. They were covered with bile and powder. I began to walk slowly up the road, the mountain above me and the plain behind me, trying to make me like them, trying to make me nothing. My palm began to itch.

I rounded a corner and saw the entrance to the cave above me, a huge black hole bursting into the rock. I stopped and looked at it for a while, feeling the heat mount around me and seeing the clouds clambering from behind the hills and pushing into the sky. I neared the entrance and stopped, thinking Alex, hoping he needed me back in the city. But everything was fine, the show was fine, it was fine. I shuddered and walked slowly towards the mouth of the cave.

It yawned about me and then I was in. The air changed and became thick with spores, hanging on me like a suit. I was in the first chamber of the cave, a high ceiling arched above me and I looked up to see that it was blackened with soot. The floor was uneven and I could feel its cold moving up into my feet. I decided to take my shoes off. I don't know why but I did and I stashed them behind a small boulder near the entrance.

I began to listen to my breath push in and out of me – my

lungs faltered and felt wary. I moved further in and the ceiling lowered; bats hung down, tight and closed like pods on some petrified tree. The air became colder. I heard the faint dropping of water as it grew heavy and yearned away from the rock. The stone was brown and cracked; in places smooth as hips, in places jagged. I began to feel tired and my arms seemed to loosen and droop from my shoulders. I laid out a line on a rock but then stood and left it, walking deeper into the cave.

I began to see shapes in the rock; an old woman's face, a rat, a small boat. Lichen moved up the walls and the roof became wetter, beaded with a curtain of droplets which caught the light sometimes and was crystal, and sometimes was dark. More green in the cave, and lilac, a lilac colour that I had never seen before. All colours in the dead rock, garden colours in the tired, heavy stone. I listened to my breathing again and it pleased me. The light began to disappear.

I turned around and looked out of the cave. I could see the imbecile plain, and beyond it the city. It was so dark around the mouth of the cave, then a circle of view and light, like a telescope. The city seemed curious, comical – smarmy and clever. I lay down on the floor, pushing my cheek on to the rock and imagining the rock breathing out colour, breathing the old red back into me. Alex tried to think me but I didn't pick up, couldn't pick up now.

I stood slowly, turned and walked deeper into the cave, pulling a light from my pocket. Stalactites grew from the ceiling. Grew? Grew? Could rock grow? It did, rock grew. Could it talk? I tested it, "Save me."

The rock answered, mimicked me; muffled and dispersed, but definitely my voice – pleading and alien in the sound mirror of the cave. I did not know if the echo was cruel or if I was awful. I walked over to a large stalactite and pressed my back on it, feeling the slime of the water and the calcite soak into my clothes. I moved my arms out behind me and held the wet rock. I could hear the patter of water. My top was wet and I took it off and dropped it on the floor.

The cave moved off in two directions, two passages gliding off into nothings. It became very important which one I chose. I moved towards one, taking its dark with my light, then I chose the other. The roof moved down and the sides came in as I walked down into the chosen tunnel. The rock was ridged and rippled like vertebrae and my head began to take on the dank chill of the cave. I pushed further in and began to shiver. I dropped my hand down and ran it along the rock as I walked, feeling it to be as smooth as my fingertips, smooth as bullet holes above a doorway in a square. Then my hand grazed against something sharp that jutted from the wall. I opened my light and bent down to look closely.

I saw brittle flecks of bone clasped in a vein of chalky rock. There was a beak and a claw – time-white shapes within indifferent wall. I snapped off the piece that pushed out furthest and put it in my mouth. It felt cool under my tongue and I pushed it forward so it rested against my teeth. I moved the bone around with my tongue, playing with it.

The roof dropped far down and I began to hear running water. I bent and continued then the cave opened into a vast space. I tried my echo and the cave replied. The voice sounded fuller and kind. I felt like I was in a huge bell.

I made to the centre of the space and sat on the floor, sensing that the cave was joined to my mind somehow, sensing that the cave and my mind were the same. I didn't know what that meant but it pleased me. I lay back and closed my eyes. I could feel the tiny veins in my eyelids walking blood across themselves. I laughed and my echoes were sweet. The sound of water continued, slapping and guzzling further off in the cave.

I lay like that for a long time and the darkness seemed to turn and pulse around me. My breath slowed now and it moved into the sound of the water. I knew that they were the same then, knew that water and breath were somehow the same. I imagined I was breathing water, that all the dark had turned to water and I was laying in the cave, waiting to be born into the plain and into nothing.

I found a sound in the cave and knew it had been waiting for me. I knew that it was not the sound of a car dying or of an eagle when it cries. I stood up and decided to take off my trousers and underwear. I lay back down and enjoyed the touch of the rock on my skin. I began to think of Cassie and imagined that she was very old and had fallen down some stairs, landing heavily at the bottom.

A drop of water fell onto my face and ran down to my neck. I listened to the sound of the blood in my ears.

I needed water. Though I didn't want to drink it; I just wanted to be near it, wanted to see it being it. I wanted water to be water. I moved around the cave, waving my light across its walls. I spotted a small opening and moved towards it. The sound of water increased. I passed through the entrance and crawled forward. The water chattered and slicked nearby. My hand passed into nothing as I put it down. I had reached a ledge. I held the light down and saw a drop beneath me; perhaps two metres, and at the bottom deep water charging round elbows of jutting rock. I sat on the ledge for a while, then flopped down into the water.

I drifted down, eyes closed, my surgery keeping me afloat. The stream grew as it was met by others. Then light ahead of me and the water racing quickly towards it. The roof above me lifted higher and higher and the light grew stronger. Then I was outside.

I lay in the stream for a while, caught in its heady silver, feeling the sun beat onto my body. I stood and looked down to the city and the plain, then climbed from the stream and walked back towards the mouth of the cave. I found my shoes behind the boulder and put them on. The line I'd laid out earlier was still on the rock and I took it into me. I walked into the road and waited for a cab that would take a naked Shaper to the city.

EIGHT

Louis was the first to awake. A bird had nested in his beard during the night and when he moved his head it fluttered up across his face and into the sky. He walked over to the far side of the pass and looked down to the city and the plain. Sadness knotted into his shoulders and made his mind dull.

Sansu and Alberto awoke next, untwining themselves and standing and stretching out. They were full of laughter and they roused the giant by dropping boulders on to his belly. Once awake, Gargantua performed eight somersaults, did six thousand four hundred and nine press-ups, then told the story of his victory over the Duke of Octalbounce. He scurried around, recreating the scene and shouting oaths so loudly that they bounced from the newly risen sun and returned a few minutes later, not as loud but definitely hotter. Sansu and Alberto laughed at Gargantua, their hands plaited together like mating spiders.

Breakfast was finished and the troubadours packed Gargantua's bag and walked across the pass with the girl cat resting sleepily on the giant's head. Alberto's tulip stood up to face the sun and he cocked his bowler hat backwards. They picked their way to the brink of the wild descent and stood for a moment, filled with the apprehension of arrival. Then they began to move; flurries of shingle moving down beneath them as they waded from the pass.

An eagle arced near them and the sun began to find their skins. They moved down for a long time, their breathing heavy and their bodies growing red and wet. Alberto was ahead, legs pushing over boulders, feet juddering down faces of scree. Next came Sansu, talking to Gargantua; then Louis, tugging his beard and walking with heaviness. Alberto paused for a moment and looked out to the city. He felt inside himself, wondering if it was too late. Gargantua began to dream of all the bars in the city and all the fine ones he'd cavort with. A dog-like happiness moved into his face and he did not notice that Sansu, a little way ahead of him, had stopped walking and stood, looking down at the plain. The giant bumped into her and she fell forwards, her cape parachuting outwards as she tumbled. Gargantua rushed towards her as she rolled down the hill. She came to a halt and stood quickly, becoming scornful and berating the giant for his absent-mindedness.

Gargantua was greatly concerned: he tapped Sansu's knees with his cat; examined Sansu's throat by prodding it with a small twig; and checked her eyesight by rushing back up the hill to hold up various combinations of fingers. Finally, he tested her memory by making her recount his victory over Lord Gretin. And though she missed the episode in which Gargantua "uselessized" the Lord's cavalry by eating their horses, he was satisfied that she remained as compos as she did mentis.

Louis had stopped his walking, not wanting to catch up with the others. He continued now and followed them down the mountain. When he reached the point at which Sansu had fallen, he spied a small object wedged between two rocks. He picked it up and examined it. It was a notebook. He turned it round in his hand and saw Sansu's name embossed in gold letters on its moleskin cover. It must have fallen from her cape as she tumbled, he thought, as he glanced towards the figures of the other troubadours. He sat down quickly, greedily opening the book.

"Two men entered my cell. Both wore masks but there was something about the smaller of the two that I recognised. The animal cunning that I had felt since the moment of my arrest reared up in me and my senses sharpened. I looked at the man and I did know him. I saw his eyes within the black of his mask and I knew him. He was one of my former students. I used to teach the man, politics at university. I had obviously failed to educate him sufficiently. They began their work on me. I vowed then that I would never describe what they did until I was stood in front of a judge. But I will say this: I had always believed that if you reached out to someone, as I had to my former student and present torturer; if you explained slowly what was happening in our country; the disappearances, the slaughter, the sickness of the power, then there would be something in them that would have to recognise that it was wrong. I had been mistaken, it was not enough. All that I had believed was shattered the first time the former student touched me.

"They released me and I returned to live with my mother and sisters. I had not told my captors anything – there was nothing to tell. They knew that. The purpose of my arrest, imprisonment and torture was, I deduced, to let me know that if there was something to know then they could know it.

"My days settled into restorative naps in the peace of my mother's garden and the lullaby of sympathy. My health began to improve, and if the hunger strike I had initiated whilst in jail had left me weak and with cheek bones like scimitars, it seemed to have had no long- term effects.

"I sat on the lawn for many days and received endless visitors, to whom I was an object of pity and curiosity. I had returned from hell. They were drawn to me as in dreams when we are drawn to what we fear the most. I reclined in my garden chair, surrounded by hushed courtiers, my existence now eloquent to them of the stoicism of the heart. My health blossomed, but I began to feel torpid, began to feel that the energy of my rejuvenation was been squandered.

"I began to resent the inertia of my entourage, and to realise that I had fallen into an insidious trap in which I saw myself as a tragic hero. I sipped my tea and they saw me as ethereal and precious, an icon like Saint Sebastian, smiling despite the arrows in his side. Their pity began to curdle within me as they mythologised my unhappiness and made me love it.

"One morning I was awoken by my own screaming. I packed my things and left my mother's house. I would not fall to being gentle and wise and defeated.

"I moved back into my rooms at the university. My persecutors believed they had made a senescent, doddering saint of me and allowed a limited freedom of movement. I mixed among my peers, the intellectuals; seeing their collaborations, how they used their erudition to mitigate; how they prospered in our wounded country. I saw that they would really do nothing.

"I awoke one day and walked from my room. I walked across the city and when I arrived at its borders I did not stop but walked out into the desert. I did not know where I was going, did not know what I was doing. It was as though I had been called by someone or had invoked the power of chance. I walked for many days across the maddening emptiness of the desert and in time began to feel a strength growing in me like a lotus or like laughter. "I realised that despite the destruction of my certainty, one tiny germ remained at the centre, one small nub of truth remained in me. It was this: whenever I came to recall my torture, whenever I thought of others who had been similarly treated, a question came into my mind; it remained the one question I was sure I could answer – 'Do I say yes to this or do I say no?' It was my pulse of black and white in my world of brittle grey. 'Do I say yes to this or do I say no?'"

Louis' hands fell to his lap and the book lay open and wide. He felt a shiver of shame at having read it without permission, but this feeling was overrun by a greater one. He snapped Sansu's book shut and stood. He looked towards the city and thought of the one they'd come to find. He let his eyes fall, sliding down the sides of the scrapers until they picked out three figures on the side of the mountain: a giant, a tiny man and a knife-thin woman.

Louis stood and began to walk down towards them, the gross weight of him lifting and moving in convection towards the pristine sky.

When he reached the figures, he handed Sansu her book and she kissed him.

9

The night had offered me little sleep, merely shuttled me between different types of fever. I climbed from bed and walked to the shower. The laughter track roared and gasped and chuckled. I broke it, ripped it out of me. There was something in me, some recklessness. I was tingling for movement. I decided to walk the city.

I surveyed my wardrobe for a long time, eyes scuttling across its many items. I laughed; real too, no track, and I selected the clothes in which I had arrived in the city. I left the flat, gliding down the leg of the elevator into the street. I began to walk towards the river.

Cabs approached me and I sent them away. I felt giddy. A cat with a girlish face came up to me, stared, then ran into an alley. The day was cool and wet, falling from dirty steel clouds and the air was thick. I looked above, saw Boundless move across the netting with automatic swings. Then I looked down at my feet, seeing my heavy boots arcing forward. The greatest of all walkers. I smiled as I moved towards the river.

The water moved slowly and crows wheeled above it. I

listened to their caws and felt scared for a moment, scared of the indifference of things. I paid an Extra and looked out again across the lumbering oil of the water. The Traders' Palace squatted on the far side of the bank, its columns reaching up into ether and delusion, and its powder blue walls gliding like a soft and cartoon sky. I thought Evan. He was in the Traders' and called me over. There was new war and he asked me in for a sortie.

Screens tumbled through my mind. I told him I'd meet him outside and paid an Intrans to row me across the water. I walked through the huge courtyard of the Traders', boots slapping puddles empty. I climbed the steps and waited, letting the dense moisture of the day depress me. Evan came out. He was hot and giddy from the sortie. He offered me a line. I didn't want.

"Thought you'd be too busy Shaping to talk to me Juan. Jesus," he looked at my clothes. "Is this what we'll be wearing tomorrow?"

I smiled at Evan, I'd always liked him. "I wanted to say goodbye." I didn't know why I said that.

"Where are you going Juan?"

I shrugged.

"The city's yours for the Shaping."

Again, I shrugged. I couldn't answer him. I didn't even know that I was leaving. Those words just came out. I didn't know what I was saying. "I have to go Evan. Goodbye." I held out my hand and Evan put his into it. We shook and I walked off.

"Juan... Juan." Calling after me through the rain. I didn't turn, just held up a hand and tilted it slightly, my knuckles facing towards him, suggesting a wave.

I thought Cassie and she took it, saying she was home.

She was cagey but she said I could come round. I walked from the centre of town, passing Kowloon Clock Tower and the Louvre and spying the molten towers of the Sagrada Familia. My clothes were wet and they clung to my body. I reached Cassie's and she thought me up. I entered her flat as she was changing. She walked up to me, kissing me on the lips, her eyes wide open. I moved away from her and sat down on the sofa. I looked at her as she stood still in the middle of the room, letting my eyes coat and touch her.

I felt bored. I had nothing to say, nothing at all to say to Cassie. I realised that I did not want her and had never wanted her. I had only wanted to want her. It all seemed so obvious to me now and for the first time I became truly aroused by her.

I stood up. I stuttered and laughed. She aimed her eyes at me, waiting; and waiting I said, "I'm sorry," and turned to walk from the flat. She followed me, close behind, running a fingertip across my shoulder and down to the canal and bone at the centre of my back. I turned to face her; she looked wounded, like a human might if they had been rejected. Her eyes were full of me now, my indifference and strangeness making her want me. I hauled myself from her and turned again, walking towards the door. I felt her look at me, felt her mouth harden and become snide as I opened the door.

Closing the door behind me, my heart echoed its slamming. I looked around me; the cheap and the closed shops, the wet and rotting buildings and the useless umbrella of the sky above them. Then I walked down the street and turned, looking up and seeing Cassie stood by the window; the two screens of her eyes behind the screen of the glass; useless as yesterday morning, two broken toys in a bored child's arms.

I rounded the corner, out of sight, and leaned against a wall, feeling its brick support my fluid skeleton. I bent down and vomited. I realised that the top of my head was missing and the sky and my mind were mating.

The clouds were ugly and dark as scabs. I loved Cassie for a moment. A cab drove past me and I pretended it was a horse, swore it was a horse. I chased it down the street telling it to giddy-up. I hated Cassie now.

The rain was loud. I headed back into town. A group of Intrans were stood outside Grand Central Station, I walked towards them and moved my baton across them, one by one. They felt my funds moving into them. I walked into the station and bought many single tickets, then I walked back outside. I handed the tickets to people, just as Alex had handed me an invitation when I had first come to the city. The rain was coming down harder now and the streets had cleared of people. I looked up to the new scrapers that rimmed the shore and I thought of my visit to the beach. I thought Sarah but when she picked up I let the line go dead.

I walked back to the flat via the museum district. The Youseum was smiling at me, it was wearing a bowler hat with a tulip wagging from it. Two stubby queues squatted in its mouth. I arrived at the flat and ascended, seeing the city multiply beneath me. Inside, and I lay on the sofa, breathing heavily. I lifted my top and looked at my breasts. I undid my fly and got my new dick out, then I walked round the flat for a while, swinging it between my legs. I entered the kitschen and opened a drawer, pulling out a fork which I took back to the sofa.

I pushed the fork against me, scoring my skin with its prongs. I jabbed it into my left breast and then my right. I squeezed them, kneading jelly out from the small holes. I wrung them dry and looked at the flaps of skin that were left on my chest. I jabbed the fork into my cock and squeezed it, letting the jelly ooze slowly from the tiny holes. The skin hung loose around it; my cock like a dwarf rummaging in a dark, collapsed tent. I lay there for a long time, feeling the jelly collect against my body. I watched the night on replay then felt tired and did some war.

Rogue channel, unauthorised footage, pictures of faces. Faces on the screen, twisted and aged with war, bombs under their eyes. Faces shouting. And behind the faces, bodies, twisted as clowns, lying in the rubble. I was shocked to feel shock move into me. I tried to move my arm and could not, I looked across at it and wondered if it was mine or if it were a clown's arm. Did it belong to one of the twisted clowns? Did it belong in blood and rubble? I tried to move it again and could not.

I felt my palm begin to ache and felt happy. I stood up and danced for a while, letting my jelly fall down onto the carpart. I watched it wobble then stain the floor, watched what was once my body melt into the floor. I jumped up and down on it.

I killed the visuals then moved into the bedroom, spreading across the Shaper-sized bed. I closed my eyes and did some dark. I began to feel calm. My breath slowed and gained rhythm. I thought Sarah again but she did not pick up. I fell asleep and when I awoke there was no light coming in from the window.

My head was full of message. Alex had been trying for a long time. He tried again but I did not take it. I lay there for a while and looked at where the dark of the room and the dark of the city touched and rubbed against each other. The window was open and the rain was heavy, bursting then collecting to run across the hardness of the city. The rain made me smile and I thought of an old smell; the musty, low smell of water on the fields and the newly wetted dust. I stood up and wrapped myself in a dressing gown, moving over to the window. Neon pursed and hung beneath me. I could make out my Alps, and below them Vesuvius.

... I blinked and saw a cloud of dark smoke rising from the volcano. Up it went, variously black, the shape of a huge and mangled tree. I saw rising showers of cinder and of stone; saw fiery ribbons lashing upwards, and burning rock pouring also over the volcano's high lips. The earth shook and a dreadful black cloud moved across the city. Lava fell from the sky into the city, just as wide steams of it rolled in after crouching across the plain. I saw the city turn to soft and sluggish stone. And the people were encased in stone, trapped in their attitudes, Medusas who had looked at themselves. And silence now in the city; just the low bubble of the molten rock and the soft fall of cinders. The stone city. The still city. I began to cry...

... Then over by the scar of yellow beach, I saw water fold upwards and begin to fall. The sea falling on the stone... A radio began to play; an engine ticked over. A finger, a hand, an arm writhed and pushed from stone; a leg now; hands came loose from netting. Stone cracked everywhere, people stepping from tombs. And the dead joined in too. The dead joined in too. There was no celebration – no joy. People broke from the stone, shrugged once, twice; maybe looked around at the wet and the sulphur of the city, then carried on. Cabs skidded down rolling streets of stone, and the nets and the shops both busy. Thought calls. Meetings. The city continued, lolling and as oblivious as a drunk...

I moved away from the window and sat on the sofa, my

lame breast skin falling down outside my gown. Alex thought me again and this time I took it.

"Juan, where have you been? You should have been in rehearsal today. We've got songs to do and I've got to brief you on the guests. Everybody was waiting. The President is angry with you. And I'm," he calmed a little, reaching for conciliatory tones, "and I'm a little disappointed."

He continued to talk. The receiver drifted away from my mind and Alex's words became a faint buzz. I looked down at my feet and I liked them for a while. Alex grew louder, "Juan, are you there? Are you listening? What the fuck is a matter with you Juan?"

I began to smile, "I don't know Alex. I don't feel too good. All my surgery has popped. It's leaked all over the floor."

"Your surgery has popped?"

"Popped. Popped. Alex. Do you know anything about Pompeii?"

"Listen Juan, I'm going to come over."

"I'd rather you didn't Alex."

"We've got a show to do. You're a Shaper, you're a star. There is more money than you can imagine in this. The President is paying us to keep him on screen, and you're flaking out on us. Didn't I..."

"Alex. Alex, I..."

"Juan..."

"I don't want the show Alex. I don't want anything."

I hung up. He thought me a few more times but I didn't pick up. And soon the sound of Alex thinking me began to please me, I began to enjoy the rhythm of the ring and the strength of the refusal – I refused him. I didn't want anything. I wanted less than nothing. I began to move around the flat, kicking some of my breast jelly in front of me. I found myself over by the lights and brought the flat to darkness, picking my way over to the sofa. I lay prone and began to feel tired and dizzy. I closed my eyes. I lay still for a long time and then a wave moved over me. I felt annihilated.

The rain came down outside but I felt as though I were in a desert with nothing but sand and heat around me, mating and forming more sand and heat; nothing everywhere but the sand and the heat and a small breeze rippling the dunes into other dunes. I felt that I was waiting for something, but I didn't know what. I felt hollow, I could tap myself and a booming sound would echo through me. But I felt that I had once been full, I felt the lightness and the itch of the recently evacuated bowel. And still the moronic stillness of waiting and the unbearable lassitude of the desert.

The hollow feeling, filling me. I closed my eyes and felt the desert. Rain fell outside and my palm was ticking. I flexed and tensed my hand and the clock juddered out. It fell to the floor and rolled towards the kitschen, spinning to a halt on its back. I pushed my finger through the hole in my palm and dabbed some blood against my lips.

NINE

Alberto was ahead as the rock levelled off to plain. Sansu, Louis and Gargantua walked behind him. Gargantua was telling how once a great fire had swept through his homeland and burned all the trees to charcoal. The birds had no boughs in which to sing, so he had grown a prodigious moustache on which the birds happily lived, singing until the forests had revived. He skipped about, dancing various jigs, the cat with the girl's face perched on his head.

This was only the beginning, he said as he tumbled and flew around Louis and Sansu. There were the miniature tigers of Slapdiladay whose leader was an ox-faced pomegranate; the battle with the rattan army of Lord Basket; the aquatic chimpanzees of Gongonu who wanted only pencils and traded these for the diamonds which grew in their arms; and of course...

Gargantua paused for a moment and looked across at Sansu and Louis. They were glazed over with his tales. To their relief, he remarked that he would pause for a while to allow them to digest the enormity of his storymanship. Louis began to think about the city's bookshops and the great reading room with the vast domed ceiling, in which the turning of a page could be heard from one end to the other, a distance of almost half a mile. He imagined himself in there, working day after day; first in, last out, sometimes contriving to stay in and study overnight by hiding beneath a desk when closing time came. He imagined the silence, the knowledge moving into him, his mind knotting and swelling into new formations under that sky of a ceiling.

Sansu did not want the city. She would prefer to lie by the side of the cairn with her much-loved husband; lie beneath the sky and watch the slice of new moon grow across the old. She would prefer to stay in the hills with the clean air around her. But she knew she had to go. She knew that struggle was needed to fill a life, to stop it from floating away. She looked down at her feet and let their swinging hypnotise her forward. She looked up and saw the rain clouds above the buildings.

Alberto was thinking of nothing. His head was still and stubborn. He was close now. It had been a long journey, but here on this plain of dust it was coming to an end. He could feel the sun over his head, but above the city he saw bulks of cloud, rain spilling onto the layers and flats and heights of concrete. He was close enough now to see the reflection of buildings on other buildings, images of glass on images of glass. And close enough now to hear the low hum of the city, the blanket of sound which would separate into clatters and voices and engines, sounds peeling off from the droning whole to become distinct and sharp. A tumble of hope and hurry moved through him.

The city loomed above them, the dense hulk of its

wetness perceptible now on their skin and its spiralling compendium of sound finding them and agitating them. They could see the scrapers over by the beach, and nearer, the lip of the Colosseum. They were in the outskirts now, moving through the burbs of the city. Without acknowledgement, the troubadours moved closer together, huddling into a defence of proximity.

The rain was on them. Sansu felt Alberto's arm slip into hers and she felt it shake. Gargantua and Louis moved closer together, and Louis was astonished to find that the giant did not speak to him, did not speak at all: there were no tales of the philosophising coconuts of the Duke of Arblemark; no stories involving sea horse cavalry or string warriors, there was nothing. This silence from Gargantua scared Louis, made him waggle his little finger in his ear, checking for blockage. He looked up at his companion. The giant looked serious now, intent, and Louis' heart began to thrash as he pondered the terrifying solemnity of Gargantua.

The giant turned to him, "Worried you there you whining Beardo. Did I ever tell you about the time..." But the words were lost as Louis jumped up and planted a grateful kiss on the gibbering giant's head.

Gargantua peeled Louis off him, stepped out into the road suddenly and raised his right hand to an oncoming cab. The driver stopped and peered at the giant. He looked frightened and tried to swerve around him. But Gargantua stepped sideways and blocked the driver's path. He approached the cab and tapped courteously on the side window, requesting it to be lowered. Hesitantly, the driver complied and the window came down.

The driver gulped and stared at Gargantua and the giant grew terse, "Are you an idiot sir? Will you take us into town?"

The driver continued to gawp and the impatient giant took his silence as a willingness to assist. Gargantua shouted to Alberto and Sansu who were slightly ahead. They turned and he waved them over and they back- tracked towards the cab. The four harlequins climbed into the cab, Gargantua crammed and huddled in the passenger seat. The driver stared in turn at each of the harlequins, a grimace bolted to his face. A queue of impatient cars grew from behind the static cab and their drivers began to beep and honk, hanging out from their windows, shouting. But the harlequins' driver opened the cab door and stepped quickly out.

Gargantua looked at the steering wheel then called after the driver, "Sir, allow me to reward you for this gracious loan."

The giant put his hand up to the cat who was nestled on his head and the cat pawed down a ruby, placing it in the giant's open palm. Gargantua tossed the ruby out of the cab window towards the driver and then climbed over, with atrocious difficulty, into the driver's seat. The cab driver picked up the ruby and ran away.

Gargantua lifted up his right arm, punched a large hole in the roof, pushed his head through it to gain a clear view, and rammed his foot on the accelerator.

The car swayed, swung and lurched forward, obeying a highway code known only to Gargantua (and to the "engineering squirrelmen of the Forest of Boom") Gargantua was assured at every turn of the correctness of his driving. This despite the accumulation of crashes that announced his progress through the city.

They drove by the side of the river and Louis saluted the Traders' Palace and remembered the glory years of the revolution; they drove around the paths of the Tuileries, disturbing flowers and lovers alike, and they drove round and round the museum district with such regularity that they began to resemble an exhibit. Everywhere they drove people stared: solitary mumbling figures stared at them; groups of sullen people stared at them; rich couples with preposterous clothing stared at them; and a short man dressed all in black with a white A perched upon his shoulder stared at them. He cursed them also when Gargantua ran over his foot. The giant turned the city into a crash.

Then Alberto spotted a flat, high above the rest, suspended only by a thin leg of glass and he guided the giant towards it.

The flat swayed slightly as the cab crashed into the lift which supported it. The troubadours stumbled from the cab, their harlequin clothing clinging to them in the heavy wet of the city. Sansu approached the bell and rang.

:

I have tried to explain it to the people who help me. But though their mouths smile, their foreheads wrinkle. They give me soup and move quickly from the room. The soup is thin and without flavour, but it is warm. They are both gone. I know that. Alex is gone now too. But sometimes I see the others. I see them in the morning, when the day is slow to take me. I lie in the room, eyes closed, listening to the rain and to the noise of the morning. I feel the should when I see them, feel something like happiness.

The figures move slowly across the plain. A tumbling giant at the rear, exchanging words with a bearded philosopher. Ahead of them, a tiny man and a tall woman leaning into each other. And at the front, a young man; green eyes in an oval face. He is dressed in a suit of harlequin pattern; his strides are long and easy. He is the greatest of all walkers. He rubs his palm slowly and looks across the land. I see now that he is not all of me. I did not know that before.

I have been somewhere dark and I was broken, but now I

have returned. Jane comes here to see me and it is love that I want now.

If you have enjoyed City of O,

please take a moment to review it at Amazon here:

https://www.amazon.co.uk/review/create-review?&asin=1838043020

For an exclusive free novella unavailable anywhere else visit

cmtaylorstory.com

ACKNOWLEDGMENTS

Primo Levi's reputation for tolerance obscures the steeliness of his oeuvre. His writing gave me the insights needed to believe in the much-vilified humanism, which, in modified form, is at the centre of what may appear to be a post-modern book.

Wole Soyinka's prison book, *The Man Died,* was an inspiration personally and some of its conclusions heavily inform the end of Chapter Seven. While the diamond-sharp insight of Marcel Mauss's *The Gift* informs Chapter Two.

There's an obvious debt to the most compendious and good-natured book in the world – Rabelais' *Gargantua and Pantagruel.* There was also liberal pilfering from Voltaire's *Candide.* Great dead French guys both.

On a more oblique level, there was guidance from certain political writings. Frederic Jameson's ideas on hermeneutics inspired the form of alternating narratives, while Raymond Williams' work fortified this inspiration. John Berger's book, *About Looking*, inspired the presentation of the war.

Thanks to Anna, again, and to Charlie Onians for sticking their oars in. And thanks to Paul Lenz and Andrew Chapman for their enthusiasm, editing, and weakness for literary larks.

Lightning Source UK Ltd.
Milton Keynes UK
UKHW022016151120
373432UK00005B/217